Danny Blackgoat: Dangerous Passage

Tim Tingle

7th Generation
Summertown, Tennessee

Library of Congress Cataloging-in-Publication Data available upon request.

© 2017 Tim Tingle

MIX
Paper from
responsible sources
FSC® C005010

Cover design: John Wincek

7th Generation
an imprint of Book Publishing Company
PO Box 99, Summertown, TN 38483
888-260-8458
bookpubco.com
nativevoicesbooks.com

ISBN: 978-1-939053-15-2

22 21 20 19 18 17   1 2 3 4 5 6 7 8 9

Contents

Contents

Chapter 1
Hand from the Coffin

Danny climbed into bed and pulled the sheet tight around his neck. It was wintertime in the barracks, and the night air was icy cold. As he drifted to sleep, he felt something crawl across his feet.

Danny sat up. He heard the soft whirring of a rattlesnake curled beneath the sheet. Ever so slowly, he lifted his legs and rolled to the edge of the bed.

But the rattlesnake was too quick. It struck Danny on the thigh and clung tight till every drop of poisonous venom shot from its fangs. Danny rolled to the floor and screamed.

"Ohhhh! Help me, somebody!"

Danny spotted a coffin lying next to him on the floor. As he moaned in pain, the lid of the coffin slowly creaked open. He held his breath and felt his heart pounding. What he saw next was the most terrifying sight of his life.

A bloody hand crawled from the coffin and reached for him.

"Noooo!" Danny shouted. The hand grabbed Danny by the shoulder and shook him hard.

"Let me go!" Danny hollered.

"Danny, wake up, son," a voice called from the darkness. Danny closed his eyes and wished this night would go away.

"Who are you?" he whispered.

"It's me. Rick," the voice replied. "You rolled out of bed, Danny. I'm guessing you had quite a nightmare, the way you were screaming and kicking."

Danny opened his eyes and sat up. "The rattlesnake?" he asked. "Where did the rattlesnake go?"

"There's no snake, Danny," Rick said. "It was all a bad dream."

"That can't be. The snake bit me. On the leg, in the same place the rattlesnake bit me before."

Rick said nothing. He gave Danny a friendly smile and waited for his young friend to understand what he had just said.

"I guess I dreamed about the coffin too," Danny finally said, "and the hand coming from it?"

"Yes." Rick laughed. "No coffin either. Danny, I think you're reliving old memories."

"Where are we?" Danny asked.

"Look around you," Rick said. "See if you remember."

Danny looked first to the ground, at the blanket curled at his feet. He saw several blankets and the shapes of sleeping men beneath them. The campsite was near a shallow arroyo, with a trickle of water snaking through the rocks.

Danny's sleeping place was under a skinny mesquite tree. He cast his gaze to the sky and spotted a thin slice of moon surrounded by bright blinking stars.

"Oh," he said. He reached for his leg and felt the scars of that long-ago snakebite. "I dreamed we were in the barracks. I feel foolish and dumb."

Rick laughed out loud and patted Danny on the shoulder. "You're neither one," he said. "You think I'd let you flirt with my daughter if you were dumb?"

Danny jumped to his feet. "I do not flirt with Jane," he said, holding his palms to the sky in a show of innocence.

"I know, Danny. You are always respectful. I just wanted to take your mind off your nightmare. Now, we have a long day tomorrow. Let's get some sleep." Rick turned to go, and Danny saw him cover his mouth to hide his laughter.

As soon as Rick was gone, Danny shook his blanket, making sure no snakes were curled up and waiting to strike. "I guess it was all a nightmare," he said to himself, as he snugged his blanket around his neck and tried to sleep. But the memories were too strong. He smiled when he thought of the shy Navajo girl with shiny black hair, Rick's daughter Jane.

The other memories, the bad ones, soon returned.

Danny remembered—on the day the soldiers came—climbing to the top of Canyon de Chelly. He looked down at his sheep grazing on the floor of the canyon. As he thought of his morning prayer, his fingers crept to the string around his neck and the pouch of corn pollen.

Danny remembered the twisting columns of smoke rising as the soldiers burned the hogans, the Navajo homes. He recalled the tight ropes that bound him together with a hundred other Navajos, forced to walk in the searing heat.

After he tried to escape, the soldiers stretched Danny across a horse like a saddle. They fed him twice a day, lifting his head and pouring water and soup down his throat. The soldiers ripped his shirt away, and his back was soon covered in blisters from the burning sun.

When the Navajo walkers arrived at Fort Sumner, he was tossed onto the bed of a supply wagon and hauled away. "He's a troublemaker," a soldier said, and he was taken to Fort Davis, a prison for Confederate soldiers captured during the Civil War.

Rick, the driver of the supply wagon, was the friendliest white man he had ever met, and Danny soon discovered why. Rick was married to a Navajo woman, Susan, and their daughter, Jane, was a year younger than Danny.

At Fort Davis, Danny was a prisoner and a Navajo, disliked by the soldiers and hated by the other prisoners.

"I'm not working with that dirty Indian," they said. The meanest of the prisoners put a rattlesnake in Danny's bed one night. Danny would have died without the help of his only friend among the prisoners, an old Southerner named Jim Davis. Davis cut the flesh of Danny's leg and sucked the blood to drain the venom. Danny shivered to think of Jim Davis with a mouthful of blood and rattlesnake venom.

With the help of Davis, Danny gained his freedom in a daring graveyard escape. But Danny's family was still imprisoned, held captive with thousands of other Navajo people in the scorching, barren land surrounding Fort Sumner.

With his nightmares and his memories over, sleep finally came to Danny Blackgoat. At the first hint of morning light, he climbed to the top of the tallest hill and lifted the leather pouch from around his neck. Danny sprinkled corn pollen onto his palm and turned to the east, to the rising sun. He closed his eyes and whispered the words his grandfather had taught him.

When the morning sun casts its light on the canyon walls
A new house is born,
A house made of dawn.
Before me all is beautiful.
Behind me all is beautiful.
Above me all is beautiful.
Below me all is beautiful.
Around me all is beautiful.
Within me all is beautiful.

Tajahoteje.
Nothing will change.

Danny opened his eyes, lifted his closed palm, and sprinkled the corn pollen on the distant rising sun.

Chapter 2
You Can't Outrun Your Past

After his morning prayer, Danny gathered wood and built a small fire to boil the water for coffee. Soon he was joined by wagon driver Rick and the Grady family.

Grady was a rancher who was left for dead by slave traders. They had killed many of his workers, captured several more, and burned his ranch house to the ground. The slave traders then took his wife and daughter, Sarah. In a daring rescue, Danny Blackgoat saved their lives, and Manny, the leader of the slave traders, was killed.

Now, Mr. and Mrs. Grady, their lively daughter, and their remaining men were returning to the Grady ranch—or what remained of it.

"What was all the ruckus about last night?" Mr. Grady asked, sipping his coffee.

"Just some misunderstanding about a rattlesnake," Rick said, staring into his coffee cup as he spoke, letting Grady know to change the subject.

"We have another long day ahead of us," Grady said, tossing the remains of his coffee to the ground and standing. "We'll stop only long enough to rest the horses."

Danny rode in silence behind Mr. Grady and his men. They rode all day and well into the night, as thin blue clouds floated across the moon. After midnight, Mr. Grady halted.

"Whoa," he said to his horse, pulling the reins and turning to face his men. "It's time we get some sleep," he said. "But before we do, I have something to tell you. I know you've been wondering what happened to the other ranch hands, your fellow workers.

"I wanted to get far enough away from Manny's hideout before I said anything about them. I was afraid some of you might want revenge and put us all in danger. Though I wouldn't blame you, we cannot raise the dead. We must consider our own safety first."

As he said "we cannot raise the dead," his ranch workers stared hard at him. The tension in the air was thick, and they waited for his explanation. He waited till they circled their horses around him.

As Danny watched, Mr. Grady opened his mouth to speak. He took a long breath and said nothing.

He is grieving for his men, thought Danny. *I know what he is thinking. If he doesn't say it, it isn't true, not yet.*

Rick rode beside him, leaned close, and said in a quiet voice, "This will never happen again, Grady. You have more friends than you'll ever know. I'm one of them."

"So am I, Mr. Grady," Danny said.

"Me too," said Williard, one of his workers.

"Same goes for me, Mr. Grady," said Vickers, another ranch worker.

"We might be your ranch hands, but you're as close to family as we've got," said a third man.

"I think you know what I'm about to say," Mr. Grady continued, looking at each of his men one by one. "Our fellow workers, all of them, are dead. Their graves are in the woods overlooking the spring. I am only alive because these two men, Rick and Danny Blackgoat, found me in the woods and saved my life."

The men moved not a muscle. The dead men were their friends and fellow ranch hands. For years they had bunked with them, shared meals with them, and fought with them to keep the wolves away. Hearing of their death, they hung their heads in silence.

"We'll camp here till sunrise," Grady said. "I'd like to get to the ranch as soon as we can."

The men tied their horses to a stout tree trunk and rolled their blankets to the ground. In less than half an hour, everyone was asleep.

As Grady and his men drifted into a peaceful sleep, a dozen United States cavalrymen slept on the other side of the same hill. While Grady told his ranch hands of the death of their fellow workers, a soldier nudged Jim Davis with his rifle and awakened him.

"Davis, sit up," the soldier said.

"What is it?" Jim Davis asked.

"You can't be very comfortable with that chain tied around your ankle," the soldier said.

"Ummm," Davis muttered. "It does make rolling over in your sleep a little hard to do."

The soldier smiled. "That's what I like about you, old man. You'd squeeze a laugh out of a bloody blanket."

"As long as I'm not in it," said Davis.

"Well, I'm unlocking that chain for you. We're so far into the desert, you'd have no place to go. Just understand, if you decide to run, we will wrap your body in that bloody blanket."

"I am too old to run, and I thank you," Davis said.

"Now let's get back to sleep, old man. We've still got a long ride to Fort Sumner."

Jim Davis rolled into his first comfortable sleep since the soldiers had left Fort Davis, a

Civil War prison camp in west Texas. Although a rebel prisoner, Davis was in charge of the carpentry shop.

Over time he gained the trust of the soldiers and officers and was able to move freely about the fort. Jim Davis was the only prisoner who became friends with the hardworking Navajo boy, Danny Blackgoat. For several months, during late-night sessions, Davis taught Danny to speak English and to begin to read.

Jim Davis even told his young Navajo friend about gift-giving at Christmas. And to prove his friendship, Davis gave him a horse and helped Danny Blackgoat escape.

As he lay on the ground and tried to sleep, Davis remembered Danny Blackgoat, the Navajo boy he had grown to love like a son. He had no way of knowing that Danny Blackgoat was asleep on the far side of the same hill.

As dawn broke and streaks of red colored the hilltops to the east, Davis stood up and slowly made his way to the top of the hill. He thought he heard something moving behind a boulder. He froze, hoping it wasn't a cougar looking to feed her young.

As he carefully leaned around the boulder to catch a glimpse of the morning prowler, Davis heard a voice—the voice of his young Navajo friend, Danny Blackgoat!

I know he is saying his morning prayer, thought Davis, *so I will wait for the prayer to be over.* As Danny sprinkled corn pollen on the rising sun and turned to the path leading downhill, Jim Davis stepped from behind a boulder to greet him.

"Good morning, Danny," he said.

After his nightmare only a few hours earlier, Danny was not ready for such a surprise. He flung himself against the boulder, with his arms stretched out beside him, as if he were clinging to life to keep from falling.

"I'm sorry," Davis said. "I didn't mean to scare you! I waited for you to finish your prayer, out of respect. But I couldn't let you leave without saying hello."

"What are you doing here?" Danny asked.

"I am traveling to Fort Sumner," said Davis. "They need a carpenter, and that's what I do best. Besides scaring you—I guess I'm pretty good at that too. Will you forgive me?"

"Jim Davis, of course I forgive you. I was afraid I would never see you again."

Chapter 3
Crossroads of Danger

"We don't have long to talk, Danny," Davis said. "Just tell me this, are you safe?"

"Yes," Danny said, "I am with friends. Rick is here, down the hill."

"Ahh, good. I am still a prisoner, and they'll come after me if I don't return to camp soon. As I said, they are moving me to Fort Sumner to help with carpentry work. Is your family still there?"

"Yes. I have seen them. They are well for now, but slave traders raid the camps at night. The water is bad. People are dying, and I am afraid for my family."

"You are smart to be afraid, Danny. Do you know the soldiers are still looking for you?"

"I know to stay hidden."

"Your life is in danger, Danny. If they catch you, they will hang you for stealing your horse, Fire Eye."

"I will be very careful when I visit my family," Danny said. "For now, I will live and work at this Grady ranch. The men I am with all work there too."

"Good. We should say good-bye now. I am very glad to know you are alive, Danny."

"You are a good man, Jim Davis," Danny said, laughing, "even though you almost made me fall from the hill."

Davis gave Danny Blackgoat a warm hug. "I will keep a lookout for your family," he said.

"Let's meet at the next full moon. If you can, slip out of the fort before sunrise," said Danny.

"Where?" Davis asked.

"There is a small cave not far from the road, on the way into the fort. Rick can show it to you."

"A good plan. See you then. Be careful, Danny."

"Oh, Jim, I should warn you," Danny said. "Sometimes rattlesnakes sleep inside the cave. So let's meet close to the cave, not in it."

"Thank you for remembering, Danny," Davis said, smiling and shaking his head. Happy to see each other alive, both Danny and Davis returned to their camps. Davis, of course, said nothing of his encounter with his Navajo friend.

When he returned to camp, one of the soldiers called out, "Where have you been, you ol' fool?"

"Doing my business and watching the sunrise," Davis replied. "Don't worry, I can't outrun a horse."

On the other side of the hill, Danny crept among the sleeping men and approached Rick.

"Rick, it's Danny. Wake up."

"What is it?"

"We should be very careful," Danny said. "The soldiers from Fort Davis are camped on the other side of this hill, just above the road. They have Jim Davis with them, and they are on their way to Fort Sumner."

"That is not good," Rick said, leaping to his feet. "My wagon is still in the woods by the roadside. It is filled with supplies for Fort Davis. I've got to beat them to it."

"Rick, you don't have to be afraid," Danny said. "Just ride into their camp and tell them where you've been. You helped rescue a mother and her daughter from slave traders. That is the truth, and you can see Jim Davis too."

"Danny Blackgoat, sometimes you are smarter than a young man should be. What was I thinking?" Rick said.

Danny shrugged his shoulders. "Maybe don't tell them I'm here," he said.

"Yeah, it's best if they don't know that, Danny." Rick did not share his thought with Danny. He knew what the soldiers would do if they caught him. *Danny Blackgoat would be swinging from the end of a rope*, he thought.

As the sun rose, Mr. Grady and his men rolled their blankets up and led their horses to a breakfast of dried desert grass. Now that they were a day's ride away from the slave trader hideout where she and her mother were held prisoner, Sarah Grady came to life.

"Mom, we should be home today!" she shouted. "We can cook a good meal for everybody. I can't wait!" Sarah was ten years old and full of fire.

Mr. Grady looked at his wife. They had avoided speaking of what life would be like, the new life, after their return.

"I have something to tell you both," Grady said. He patted the ground beside him, and his wife and daughter sat by his side. "Since they knocked me out and left me for dead, I don't know how much you saw."

"It was bad, Dad," Sarah said. "Those men were mean."

"You know they set fire to the house and barn?" Grady asked.

"Yes," Mrs. Grady said, "and I expect they killed most of our cattle too."

"The cattle are scattered," Grady said, "but if they found their way to the springs, they might still be alive."

"We are alive," said Mrs. Grady, "and that is a miracle. We have much work to do, but we've done it before."

"I am grown up now," Sarah said. "Me and Danny Blackgoat can rebuild the ranch!"

Danny was walking nearby and overheard the conversation.

We can let the others help us if they want to, he thought.

The Gradys, the ranch hands, and Danny saddled their horses. Rick lifted himself to his wagon seat and snapped the reins.

"We should be there in a few hours," shouted Mr. Grady. He glanced at his wife and saw the worried look on her face.

No one spoke as they neared familiar ground. Everyone climbed into their own world of remembering the good days—and dreading what they would see.

Four hours later, as they neared the Grady ranch, they eased their horses into a slow walk. Danny patted Fire Eye on the neck and stroked his mane.

"We're almost home," he whispered, then closed his eyes at the mention of home. *Will I ever see my home again?* he thought.

Chapter 4
Shotgun Surprise

As they topped the hill overlooking the Grady ranch, Danny was glad it was noontime. *If we returned at night*, he thought, *the ranch would look like a wide desert of fire, unsafe for life. The fires burn quieter now, in the heat of day.*

As Danny eased Fire Eye over the hill, the feisty pony spotted the spring of cool water below. He snorted, shook his head, and took off in a gallop that caught Danny by surprise.

"Whoa, boy!" Danny said, patting his neck and pulling on the reins. But Fire Eye only slowed enough to skid a few feet down the hill, then continued running. Danny laughed and let him run. Fire Eye splashed into the spring, turning circles in the water.

"Fire Eye!" Danny shouted. "Slow down!"

Clinging to his horse's neck, Danny leapt from the saddle into the shallow waters of the spring. The water was above his knees, but Fire Eye stomped and splashed his front and rear legs both, dancing in the chilly waters and drenching Danny's clothes.

For a brief moment Danny was angry, but Fire Eye was overjoyed—after so many hours of desert sand—to finally feel the cool waters of a fresh spring. Danny put his hands on his hips and glared at his horse. Fire Eye paused and took a few steps in his direction. Danny stood still and waited. Fire Eye bowed his head, as if he understood how wrong it was to soak his friend to the skin.

"You're a good horse, Fire Eye," Danny said, reaching out and petting Fire Eye between the ears. But Fire Eye wasn't finished. He dipped his head in the water, flung it at Danny, and hit him in the face with a huge wave.

"Ohhhh," Danny yelled, covering his face with his hands. He turned to the woods and dashed to the shore. He was about to step into the woods when he heard a man's voice in front of him, in the shadow of the trees.

"Don't I know you, boy?" the man said in a mean and threatening voice. In the glare of the sun, Danny saw the reflection of a gun barrel. When he heard the click of a rifle, he knew his life was in danger.

He leapt into the water, and the *pow* of a shotgun blast shattered the quiet morning. Fire Eye reared up on his hind legs and flashed his hooves. A soldier stepped from the woods and aimed once more at Danny.

"I know you!" the soldier shouted. "You're that Indian boy from Fort Davis. You thought you got away!"

With shotgun shells exploding around him, Danny dashed through the shallow water. He slipped into the woods away from the soldier, and Fire Eye ran beside him. Watching the scene below, Rick picked up his own shotgun and aimed at the soldier.

"You've killed your last Navajo," Rick whispered. He lifted the gun to his shoulder and squinted his eyes, taking careful aim. He felt a hand on his shoulder and looked to see Grady.

"Shoot to scare him," said Grady. "If you kill a soldier, our lives are over."

Rick nodded and took aim at a tree stump near the soldier's feet.

Pow!

He fired his shotgun and the tree stump blew apart, showering the soldier with splinters and shards of wood. The soldier dropped his shotgun and fell to the ground. His hands flew to his face, wiping his eyes of debris.

With the blast still ringing in his ears, he scrambled to his feet and dashed to the woods.

"Keep your gun ready," said Grady. "When he realizes he doesn't have his shotgun, he'll make a run for it. Just be sure you don't hit him."

"Thanks for the reminder," Rick said. "Anyone that shoots at Danny has me to answer to. He saved my life, and I'll never forget it."

"He saved mine too," Grady said. "But we have a big problem."

"What?"

"The soldier didn't walk to get here. He was probably riding by and saw the smoke. His horse is in those woods," Grady said, pointing below. "And he's on horseback right now, I'll bet, looking for Danny. He might even get a promotion if he brings back that Indian boy who escaped from the fort."

"And they'll take him dead or alive," said Rick, "because that Indian boy is a horse thief."

"Any ideas?" Grady asked.

"I've got one, Daddy," a sweet little voice replied. All eyes went to Sarah. "Let's stop talking and save Danny!"

Grady gave his daughter a look of pride, but only for a moment.

"Let's go!" he shouted to his men. "Williard, take two men and circle the woods to the east. Vickers, you and your men circle to the west. We'll meet at the ranch house!"

"I'm gonna ride straight down the hill and wait at the tree stump," Rick said. When

Grady gave him a curious look, Rick said, "I know Danny Blackgoat. He'll do the last thing anyone would expect him to do. He knows he can't outrun the soldier on horseback. He will hide out, let the soldier ride past him, and meet Fire Eye where all this trouble started, at the tree stump."

"You take care of Danny," Grady said, "and I'll take care of the soldier." He looked at his men, who huddled nearby waiting for orders.

"Let's go!" he called out, waving his arm forward.

The two groups rode and skidded their way down the hill in opposite directions. Rick and Grady drove their horses straight to the tree stump, crossed the spring, and pulled to a halt.

"Hello, soldier. Are you there?" Rick asked. "I drive a supply wagon for the US Army, and I heard shooting. Are you all right?" When no one answered, they rode into a thick clump of trees.

Grady stepped from his horse and picked up the soldier's shotgun. "I'm going for him,"

Grady said. "I'll return his rifle and tell him my men were shooting at the Indian boy. I'll keep him gone long enough for you to get Danny up the hill. Hide him in the back of your wagon."

"Good plan," Rick said, "if we can catch Fire Eye."

"Danny Blackgoat will catch Fire Eye. No worry there," said Grady.

"Then I'll tie him to the wagon. We can tell the soldier I'm bringing the horse to the fort."

"Which fort?" Grady asked.

"Whichever fort he's not going to," Rick said, laughing. "You know Danny's not letting me take his pony from him, after all they've been through."

Grady nodded good-bye to Rick and rode after Danny, hoping to reach him before the soldier did. Rick and Grady had the same fearful thought at the same time.

What if he's not the only soldier in the woods?

Chapter 5
Hide-and-Seek Conversation

Grady and his horse knew these woods. They knew the fastest riding paths through the trees and scrub bushes. Soon Grady spotted the soldier, sitting on his horse and gazing through the trees for any sign of "the Indian boy."

Grady didn't hesitate. He approached the soldier and spoke.

"Have you seen the Indians?" he asked.

The soldier jumped as if hit by a lightning bolt. He turned to face Grady with big eyes and fear written all over his face. "Who are you?" he stammered, trying to regain his confidence. "Why are you here?"

"I'm Bill Grady and I own this ranch," he said. "I saw an Indian boy and thought there might be more. I shot at him, but I'm afraid I missed pretty bad."

"Was it you who shot the tree stump?"

"Yes," Grady said. "I'm sorry about that. Here's your shotgun. Have you seen any sign of the boy?"

"I thought I had him," said the soldier, nodding a thank-you and reaching for his gun. "I know he can't be far. His horse took off the other way."

His horse took off after Danny, thought Grady. *And they're both a long way from here by now.*

"What brings you this far from the fort?" Grady asked. "And where's the rest of your unit?"

"They rode over to the ranch house, looking for survivors," said the soldier. "I am Sergeant Blaylock from Fort Davis, Texas. We are looking for a gang of slave traders. They seem to be getting bolder. A few weeks ago they attacked Fort Sumner, and we've been called to drive them out."

"Maybe that Indian boy escaped from the slave traders," said Grady.

"Oh no, not him," said the sergeant. "I know that boy. He's a Navajo, a real troublemaker. He escaped from Fort Davis."

"Maybe it's not the same boy," said Grady.

"Oh, it's him," said the sergeant. "I'd know him anywhere. Since he was a prisoner, we cut his hair short. He's the only Indian boy around with hair shorter than yours. And when you talk to this boy, he stares right back at you. He lets you know he might do what you say, but he doesn't like it."

"How is that different?"

"These Indian kids, boys and girls both, they never look at you," said the sergeant. "They just nod their heads and do what you tell them. They show some respect. But not this one. He also stole a pony, so I'm not looking to capture him."

"What do you mean?" asked Grady.

"I want that boy dead," Sergeant Blaylock said. "Save us all a lot of trouble when he's rotting in the ground."

Grady felt his heart pound and the blood rush to his face. He hung his head and pulled his hat low to hide his anger. Sergeant Blaylock was talking about the young Navajo man, Danny Blackgoat, who saved his life.

"I'm sure he'll get what's coming to him," Grady said. *I pray he will get what he deserves*, he thought to himself.

Soon they were joined by a lieutenant and two cavalrymen.

"You all right?" the lieutenant asked. "We've been looking for you. We heard gunshots."

"Yes, I'm fine," said the sergeant. "This is the owner of the ranch, Mr. Grady. We're looking for that runaway Navajo boy from the fort."

"You saw him?" asked the lieutenant.

"Yes, and we've been taking shots at him," said the sergeant, "but he got away."

"Well, there's nothing we can do here," said the lieutenant. "Mr. Grady, looks like your ranch is burned to the ground."

"That gang of slave traders did that," Grady said. "They took my wife and daughter too. That's where we've been. During the gun battle to get my family back, we killed their leader, a fellow they call Manny."

"You killed Manny?" the lieutenant asked. "We've been after him for two years."

"We left him dead, and his men didn't seem to mind that much. Almost like he held them captive too," Grady said.

"Sounds to me like you've done our job for us," the lieutenant said. "If you'd like, my men and I can stay for an extra day and give you a hand."

"I'd sure appreciate it," Grady said. "You can help me gather together what's left of my cattle."

"We'll be glad to. We can work all day tomorrow and leave early the next morning." The lieutenant turned to Sergeant Blaylock and said, "Sergeant, take these men and see if that Navajo boy left any trail. Fire your gun in the air if you find him, and we'll join the chase."

"I'll get my family and men and meet you at the house," Grady said. The last thing he wanted were soldiers prowling around his ranch, but Grady trusted Rick. He knew if he gave him enough time, Rick would catch Danny and Fire Eye and be on his way to Fort Sumner, with Danny hidden in the back of his wagon.

"See you there," the lieutenant said. He jerked on his reins and led his horse in a slow trot to the ranch house.

Grady rode to the tree stump, hoping Rick, Danny, and Fire Eye were well on their way down the road. He paused briefly at the stump, and a slow smile crept across his face. At the base of what remained of the stump, someone had arranged bits of bark in a simple note.

O K

"Yes," Grady said aloud. "You are okay, Rick—you and Danny Blackgoat both. You risked your lives to save my wife and daughter." He turned his horse uphill, where his family and ranch hands waited.

"Did anyone see Rick and Danny Blackgoat?" he asked.

"Yes," Sarah said. "I saw Danny. He was riding Fire Eye and they took off running. Someday I want to ride a pony as fast as Fire

Eye. Dad, maybe for next Christmas instead of a new dress can I have a new pony, a really fast pony, not one for little girls, but for a grown-up girl like me, 'cause you know I will be grown up by that time."

Everyone waited patiently for Sarah to take a breath. When she finally did, Mr. Grady ignored her question. "Before we return to the ranch house," he said, "we will stop and pay our respects to the men buried in the woods."

No one spoke as they rode slowly down the hill and crossed the spring. When they came to the stone graveyard in the woods, they stepped from their horses and circled the graves.

With his family safe and the concerns of the day over, Grady hung his head and felt tears roll down his cheeks. His men took their hats off and closed their eyes, many weeping as well.

"Dear Lord," Grady said, "welcome these good men into a place of everlasting peace, if it be thy will. We will never forget the good work they did here on earth. May they find peace in a better place and help those in need."

Rick and Danny were already riding their ponies and speeding down the road to Fort Sumner. They stopped at the spot in the woods where Rick had left his wagon, almost a week ago now. Soon Fire Eye was tied to the rear of the wagon, and Danny rode on the wagon bed.

"I think you know what to do if we pass anyone on the road," Rick told him.

"Yes," Danny said. "I climb under the blanket and don't move till you say it's safe."

"That's right, Danny. Just do what I say, even if you start seeing my daughter, and we'll get along fine."

"That is not funny, Rick."

"I didn't mean for it to be," said Rick.

Chapter 6
Bridge-Builder Rick

"How far to the fort, Rick?" Danny asked.

"We should be there sometime tomorrow, if we don't run into any more trouble," Rick said.

"The soldiers will be looking for me, won't they?"

"Yes, Danny. Your life is in danger, more than ever. They know you are running free, and they know you will try to see your family."

"Will they follow Jim Davis when he comes to see me?"

"If I was looking for you, Danny, that's what I would do."

"He will be in trouble, too, if they catch us together," Danny said. "Will you warn him?

Tell him just to wait and don't try to meet me at the full moon."

"That's smart of you, Danny. The time will come. You'll just have to wait."

Danny curled under his blanket and soon was fast asleep, dreaming of his home at Canyon de Chelly. He laughed in his sleep at the sight of Crowfoot, his favorite little sheep that waddled when he walked.

As the clouds gathered in a darkening sky, Danny rolled to the rear of the wagon. Drops of rain fell softly on his cheeks. He lay half awake and half asleep.

"Crowfoot," he whispered, holding out a handful of grain. "Come here." Suddenly, the earth shook and Danny fell to the ground. His little friend floated over him. Danny moved his hands to his face and felt the raindrops, but when he looked at his hands, his fingertips were covered in blood.

"Help!" he shouted.

"Wake up, Danny," Rick said. "Another nightmare?"

"Yes," Danny said, sitting up and rubbing his eyes and staring at the moon and stars overhead. "I need to see my grandfather. He can heal me and stop these bad dreams."

"I have great respect for your grandfather, Danny," Rick said. "Now, let's get settled down for the night."

He climbed to the front seat, snapped the reins, and led the mules to a small clump of trees by the roadside.

Soon Rick and Danny were rolled up in their blankets on the ground.

"Good night, and no more nightmares, Danny Blackgoat," Rick said.

"What if I dream of your daughter, Jane, and she doesn't like me?" Danny said. "That would be a nightmare." Right away he wished he hadn't said it.

"Most of your nightmares are not real, Danny. Maybe get some sleep," Rick said, laughing.

Danny slept the remainder of the evening with no nightmares, and long before sunrise he and Rick were once more on the road to Fort Sumner. With the first hint of crimson on the clouds to the east, Rick looked over his shoulder.

"You awake, Danny?" he asked.

"Yes, for a long time."

"Whoa," he said, pulling on the reins and easing the mules to the roadside. "We can take a little break if you want to, Danny."

"Thank you, Rick," Danny said, stepping from the wagon. He climbed a nearby hill and said his morning prayer, tossing corn pollen to the sky.

When he returned to the wagon, Rick handed him a strip of dried beef and patted him on the shoulder. "I am proud of you, son," he said. "And I'll do my best to keep you safe. We need to remember, both of us, that the soldiers know you are close by. They'll do everything they can to catch you. I hate to say this, Danny, but they won't wait to watch you hang. These men will shoot you dead first and bring your body back to Fort Davis."

"They'll sling my body over a horse so I won't bloody up their wagon," Danny said.

"You know how that feels, don't you?" Rick asked.

"I rode for days like the saddle on a horse," said Danny. Without thinking, he ran his hands over his back, over scars of his blistered, wrinkled skin.

"We cannot let our guard down, not ever, if we want to live."

"They won't hurt you, Rick," Danny said.

"They will if they find out I'm helping you escape," said Rick. "Besides, I have many enemies among the soldiers."

"Why?"

"I married a Navajo woman, Danny."

"Why do the soldiers hate us?" Danny asked.

"I wish I had the answer," said Rick. "I know what they say. The soldiers say you are savages, and that allows them to do anything they want to your people."

"I never saw a Navajo kill an old man and lay his body by the roadside for everyone to see."

"People are afraid, Danny, of anyone different. My wife was afraid of me for the longest time. I never thought I'd win her trust."

"How did you do it?"

Rick drove without speaking for a long moment, snapping the reins and whistling at his mules. Just when Danny was convinced the conversation was over, Rick took a long breath and patted him on the knee.

"I was kind to her, Danny. I treated her with respect. While the soldiers barked orders at her—knowing she didn't understand a word they were saying, not at first—I spoke to her."

"You said simple words to her, didn't you?" Danny asked. "You pointed and made shapes with your hands so she could understand. That's what Jim Davis did for me when he was teaching me English."

"That's right, Danny. You understand too much for a little boy," Rick said, with a serious look on his face.

"I'm a little boy that's about to save your life," Danny said. Before Rick could reply, Danny leapt to the rear of the wagon and climbed under a blanket. "Soldiers are coming," he said.

"What! Where?" Rick said, startled into action. He jerked the reins and the mules stomped and whinnied. "Where are they?" he asked, standing to look over his shoulder. "I don't see anyone, Danny."

From under the blanket, Danny pointed to the trees by the roadside. Rick saw a flock of birds disturbed by something and soaring across the desert.

"The birds didn't fly away when they saw us coming," Danny said. "They saw something that scared them. I am guessing it's soldiers."

"Danny Blackgoat," Rick whispered to himself, "you are an amazing young man."

Soon a cloud of dust rose from the road a mile behind them. When the dust cleared, Rick saw a small platoon of soldiers, twenty or more, coming over the rise in the road. He pulled his wagon to the roadside."

"Easy, boys. Take it easy," he said to the mules. "They'll be gone soon." He started to warn Danny, but then realized Danny had already warned him. "I guess you're smarter than a mule," he said.

"I am if you're the mule," Danny replied.

Chapter 7
By Bullets or Hanging?

The next half hour became the worst nightmare Rick had ever experienced. But this was no nightmare. This was real. The soldiers did not ride by without stopping, as expected. They approached Rick as if he were the man they were looking for.

The officer in command waved his arm at his men and shouted, "Surround the wagon and shoulder your rifles!" The soldiers, still on horseback, circled the wagon and pointed their rifles at Rick.

"I work for the army," Rick said to the officer. "This is a supply wagon. I'm on my way to Fort Sumner."

"We know who you are," the officer replied. "You're Rick, and you're married to a Navajo woman. We suspect you of treason." Rick said nothing in reply.

"What supplies are you carrying?" asked the officer.

"Nothing," Rick said. "I'm on a return trip from Fort Davis."

Ignoring Rick, the officer pointed to one of his men. "Corporal, see what's under that blanket."

"Wait!" shouted Rick, standing and waving his arms at the soldiers. "There is nothing in my wagon but food supplies for my trip. Stay out of my wagon."

The officer pointed slowly to Rick, his jaw set in a look of anger.

"Ready!" he shouted.

All twenty of the soldiers lifted their rifles and aimed at Rick.

"Aim," said the officer. The soldiers placed their fingers on the triggers.

Rick lowered his arms to his sides. In the long silence that followed, he turned his head, pleading with the soldiers, staring deep into their eyes. What he saw terrified him. The soldiers wanted more than anything to fire their guns and watch him die. Rick placed his palms on top of his head and pulled his chin to his chest.

"Lower your rifles," the officer said, satisfied that Rick fully understood who was in charge. "Now, see what's under the blanket."

"I am sorry, Danny," Rick whispered to himself. "I could not save your life."

"There is nobody here, sir," a soldier said. "He is telling the truth. Nothing but supplies, food, and clothing."

Rick lifted his head and tried not to show his surprise on his face. The officer was disappointed. He tightened his lips and spat on the ground. "Show him what we had planned for him and the boy both," he said.

The corporal lifted two thick hanging ropes from his saddle.

The officer pointed to a leafless tree by the road. "My hope was to hang you two and leave your bones for the buzzards. Your skeletons would swing on that tree limb as a warning to everyone who passed by—do not help the savages."

"I understand," said Rick.

"You'd better," the officer said. "We will see you at Fort Sumner." He turned to his men and shouted, "Get ready to ride!"

They soon rode away, leaving Rick standing in the wagon and choking on the dust from their horse's hooves. As they topped the hill, he gazed at the sky, waiting for someone to appear and tell him what had just happened.

"I think it's safe now, Danny," Rick said, sobbing as he spoke. "Are you there? Are you still alive? Maybe we are both dead. Maybe. What is happening, son?"

The silence was broken only by the beating of wings, as the birds returned to their nests. "Please say something, Danny. Let me know where you are."

"Are you sure it's safe?" Danny's soft voice rose from beneath the wagon.

"Danny Blackgoat!" Rick jumped from the wagon and fell to his knees. He saw Danny clinging to the front wagon axle.

"I couldn't hold on much longer," he said. "I don't know what I would have done if they shot you."

"Danny," Rick said. "I think I know what your life has been like for the last year. I have never been so scared in my life." He took a long breath and wiped the tears from his face. "But don't climb on the wagon. Not yet. Let's sit under the trees for a while."

He led the mules to the shade of a scraggly clump of mesquite trees. Danny rolled a bundle of straw from the rear of the wagon to feed the mules. Rick nodded a silent thank-you and leaned against the trunk of the stoutest tree. He bowed his head and wrapped his arms around himself till his whole body shook.

When Rick finally opened his eyes and took a breath, Danny hurried to the wagon, returning with a bag of dried beef sticks, a canteen, and two cups.

After pouring a cup of water for himself and Rick, Danny stood tall and lifted his cup to the sky.

"I would like to offer a toast," he said.

"What? What are you doing, Danny Blackgoat?" Rick asked.

"I'm doing something I have never done before," said Danny. "But I saw Jim Davis offer toasts, and Mr. Grady too. So now, I want to offer a toast."

"Fine," Rick said. "What are you toasting?"

"Life," said Danny. "I am offering my toast to a long life for my friend Rick."

"I'll drink to that!" Rick said, nodding and raising his glass to his lips.

"I would like to offer a toast as well, Danny. Do you mind?"

Danny shrugged his shoulders and sat down. No white person had ever asked his permission before.

Rick rolled to his knees and slowly stood, while Danny filled both of their cups.

"This toast is for you, Danny," Rick said, as he held his cup to the sky. A single ray of sunshine peeked through the clouds, and Rick closed his eyes and nodded at the blessing from the heavens.

"I offer this toast to the long and happy marriage of my daughter, Jane, to the finest young man I have ever met, Danny Blackgoat of the Navajo people."

Danny was so surprised he almost dropped his cup.

"Will you drink to it?" Rick asked.

Danny's mind raced with Navajo tradition—who must give their permission, the proper way of arranging a marriage.

"I will do everything I can," he said, staring into his cup, "to make this happen. I would be honored to marry your daughter, Jane."

Chapter 8
Road to Nowhere

Rick and Danny rode without speaking for most of the afternoon. Several times Rick glanced at Danny, riding behind him in the open wagon bed. *It's nice to get that wedding idea out in the open*, he thought to himself.

As they approached Fort Sumner, Danny's mind burned like a wildfire with thoughts of the dangers ahead. He had been gone so long without hearing from his family, and now Jim Davis would be living at Fort Sumner.

I hope they are all still alive, he thought. *If the soldiers follow Jim Davis and catch us talking, will they hurt my family?*

As the sun sank below the mountains to the west, Rick pulled the mules to a halt. "Danny," he said, "the fort is only a few miles away. If we camp out here, we'll have to find a place for you to hide in the light of morning. Can you find your cave from here?"

"Yes," Danny said. "It's not far."

"Put together enough food and water for several days for yourself. You can hide out near the cave tonight, and I'll drive on to the fort. The soldiers will be less likely to look for you after dark, so we should be safe."

Danny filled a sack with dried meat and fresh water. "Rick, will you tell Jim Davis about the drinking water? People who drink it are dying."

"I'll warn him," Rick said. "Now, you be careful and take no chances. Here's a plan. If you see myself or Jim Davis come looking for you, don't run out of hiding right away. If it's a trick and the soldiers are watching, we will button our shirts tight at the collar. I'll tell Jim. That will be our sign, our warning for you to stay away. Understand?"

"Good idea," Danny said. "I've never seen you button your collars at the neck, but the soldiers won't think anything of it."

"That's what I'm hoping, Danny. But be very careful who you trust."

"Rick, will you do something for me?" Danny asked.

"Of course. What?"

"Would you ask your wife if she would be all right, if she would mind . . ." Danny hung his head, embarrassed to continue.

Rick smiled. "Come here, son," he said. He pulled Danny close to his chest and gave him a warm hug. "You want me to ask my wife if she is all right with you marrying our daughter?"

Danny nodded, still staring at the ground.

"What would you say if I told you it was her idea?" Rick asked.

"That would make me very happy," Danny said.

"Then be happy, Danny Blackgoat. Be happy and careful both."

Without another word, Danny leapt from the wagon and disappeared into the moonglow of early evening.

"Be happy and careful both," Rick repeated, whispering the prayer to himself.

Danny climbed over a small hill, crouching as he moved in case any soldiers were nearby. *The sun is down but the moonlight casts shadows*, he thought.

He circled the cave and settled in a small grove of bushes, watching the cave for any sign of life. "The rattlesnakes will always be there," he whispered.

After the long day of travel and trouble with the soldiers, Danny was more tired than he thought, and he nodded off to sleep. He was soon startled to hear a bugle call, echoing across the lake waters from the fort.

He jumped to his feet before realizing that was a very dangerous thing to do. He flopped face-first to the ground, breathing hard and casting his eyes back and forth from one hillside to the next, as if he were under attack.

Assured that no one had discovered him, Danny dusted the desert sand from his shirt and pants. Facing the morning sun, he whispered the Diné prayer and tossed his corn pollen to the sky.

"I must be careful," he said aloud, "but I must also remember why I have returned to Fort Sumner. My family needs me. I have come to rescue my family." Curious to see what lay below the fort walls, to the west, Danny tied his food and water sack around his waist and began the long walk around the lake. "We can never escape on the roads. I must find a path through the canyons and hills."

By midmorning he climbed a steep hillside and entered a thick forest overlooking the fort. *This must be a lookout spot for the slave traders*, he thought. The ground beneath the trees was covered with horse tracks, the remains of campfires, and piles of dried horse dung.

I was right, he thought, *and I must leave no sign that I was here.*

Suddenly he heard men approaching, and he knelt down at the base of a tree, hoping the riders would not enter the woods. When they passed by, he peered over the hill and spotted two soldiers, a sergeant and a private, guiding a small, open wagon. They topped the hill and led their horses down a rocky wagon road.

Where are they going? Danny asked himself. The road came to a sudden end, with no building in sight, no corral or reason for being there. "A road to nowhere," he whispered.

A cold shiver crept down his spine as he saw what the wagon carried. Two coffins.

Chapter 9
What Was He Thinking!

The soldiers parked at the road's end and dragged a long wooden box to the rear of the wagon.

"Can you lift it?" asked the sergeant.

"Not by myself," said the private. "It's too heavy. Must be one big Indian inside."

"Let's drag him over there and bury him," the sergeant said, pointing to a mound of dirt among dozens of stone markers. The soldiers carried the coffin to the gravesite, along with two shovels, and began to dig.

"A graveyard," Danny whispered. "This is very bad. The first day of my journey to rescue my family, and I stumble across a graveyard."

He lay on his back and remembered the long night in the graveyard at Fort Davis, when he lay in the coffin. Without thinking, he stretched his hands behind his back, half-expecting to feel the body of Jim Davis.

A slow smile crept across his face as he remembered how afraid he was. *But I came out of the coffin alive. Jim Davis was alive, and now we're both here at Fort Sumner. Maybe this is a good sign.*

He rolled on his belly and crept to the top of the hill, watching and waiting for his chance.

"We better take that empty coffin back to the carpentry shop," the sergeant said. "We were supposed to pick up two bodies, but one of 'em hadn't died yet."

"Have you seen that new carpenter work, the one from over at Fort Davis?" asked the private. "I heard he's a rebel prisoner."

"Yes, he's a rebel," said the sergeant, "but a hardworking one. I've never seen anyone take a pile of boards, a saw, and some nails, and throw a coffin together in a few hours. We'll be bringing this extra coffin back to his shop."

They are talking about Jim Davis, thought Danny. *They are going to Jim Davis's shop when they leave the graveyard. This is my chance to see my old friend.*

"Seems like a waste of good boards to me," the private said. "Don't know why we can't throw these Indians in a pit like we used to."

The sergeant said nothing, and the two dug the hole in silence. They lowered the coffin into the ground and began tossing dirt into the hole.

"I never did like graveyards," said the private. "Let's get out of here."

"Hold on," said the sergeant. "My old man was a preacher, and I can't leave this man without a prayer."

The soldiers stood facing the grave, with their backs to Danny Blackgoat. They held their hats in their hands and bowed their heads.

Just like the Gradys do before they eat their meals, thought Danny. *I hope they pray as long as Mr. Grady does.*

Keeping a careful eye on the soldiers, Danny crawled over the hill and dashed to the wagon.

Without a sound he climbed onto the wagon bed, lifted the lid of the extra coffin, and slipped inside. Very quietly he lowered the lid, holding his breath and hoping the soldiers saw nothing.

Once inside, he opened his mouth wide and took a deep breath. *What did I just do?* he asked himself. *I was safe. No one knew I was anywhere near Fort Sumner. And the first time I hear anybody talk about Jim Davis, I crawl in a coffin on the chance that I might get to see him! What am I doing?*

But he could not stop himself from smiling. *I know what I will do. I can play a trick on Jim Davis. Yes!*

The soldiers climbed to the wagon as if nothing had happened. "Now that we have a good carpenter," the sergeant said, "he's gonna keep us busy. No more rotting bodies on the ground."

"I still think it's a waste of good lumber," said the private.

"Well, that's not our business. Let's get back to the fort," the sergeant replied, snapping the ropes and calling to the horses. "Let's go, boys."

Inside the coffin Danny bounced from one side to the other as the wagon climbed the rocky road. As they neared the top of the hill, the road took a steep upturn. Danny felt the coffin slide a few feet to the rear of the wagon.

"Please, no," he whispered.

The horses whinnied, and the sergeant snapped the ropes again. "Come on, let's go, boys!"

Soon the wagon topped the hill and faced a long downhill path. With the extra weight, the coffin slid hard against the wagon seat.

"Hey," shouted the private. "What's going on with that coffin? It didn't slide around on the way up here." Danny clenched his fists tight and dug them into his cheekbones.

"We didn't drive as fast on the way up," the sergeant said. "We had two coffins, remember? And one of them had a body inside."

Danny relaxed and whispered a Navajo thank-you.

In half an hour the wagon came to a halt.

"Let's carry this coffin inside the shop and get some lunch," the sergeant said.

Oh, no, thought Danny. *They'll lift the coffin from the wagon and know somebody is inside. I am a dead man!*

The door to the carpentry shop opened, and a familiar voice called out, "I thought you needed two coffins." It was Jim Davis.

"Help me, please, Jim Davis," Danny whispered. "Your friend Danny Blackgoat needs you."

"Here," Davis said, as if he had heard the plea of his young friend, "let me carry that."

"It's heavy," said the sergeant.

"It is an empty coffin," Jim Davis replied. "If I can't carry an empty coffin, then maybe I need to build one for myself!"

The soldiers laughed while Davis reached over the sideboard and slid the coffin to the rear of the wagon. "You're right," Davis said. "This coffin is heavy. Feels like something is in it."

"Not unless a body crawled inside when we weren't looking," the private said, laughing.

He knows something is inside, Danny thought. In an instant Jim Davis opened the lid of the coffin and stood staring at his young friend, Danny Blackgoat.

"Anything wrong?" asked the sergeant.

Davis could not take his eyes away from Danny, with his arms wrapped tight around himself and a terrified look on his face.

Chapter 10
Back Home at the
Carpentry Shop

Danny unrolled his right fist and gave Davis a childlike wave.

"What is it?" asked the sergeant. "Some animal crawled in there and died?"

The next words I say can mean life or death for Danny, Davis thought. "Uh, no, nothing," he stammered. "Except you're gonna have to dig up every body in that graveyard. At least the ones buried in the coffins I made."

The sergeant jumped from the wagon. "What are you talking about?" Davis closed the lid and stood between the coffin and the sergeant.

"This coffin is full of mud and dirt," Davis said. "I must not be nailing 'em tight enough. They get a little rain, and they fill up with mud."

"Is this some kind of a joke?" the sergeant said, stepping around Davis and reaching for the coffin lid.

"No, no joke. I'm just gonna have to do a better job." He put a strong hand on the lid and dragged the coffin inside the carpentry shop. Then he stepped outside, carefully closing the door behind himself, and turned to the soldiers. "This is not your worry," Davis said. "I just have to do some rebuilding."

"Well, we are sure not digging up any Indian bodies just because they got a little muddy," said the private. "Let 'em drown!"

The sergeant stood silent, looking at Jim Davis and wondering what was happening. "Come on, Sergeant. Let's go get some lunch," said the private, snapping the reins.

The sergeant shook his head and climbed into the wagon. He glanced over his shoulder as if about to say something to Davis, then decided against it. "Let's go," he called to his horses.

Davis stood at the doorway, waving at the soldiers till they rode out of site.

"You sure know how to bring a little excitement into a man's life, my friend," he said, closing the door behind him.

"Can I come out?" Danny asked.

"Gimme a minute to lock the door. And make some coffee. You got some explaining to do."

"What if the soldiers come back?"

"I guess you still have that good strong Danny Blackgoat brain," Davis said. When he opened the coffin again, he had a big grin on his face. He reached down and pulled Danny out of the coffin.

"Bring me the broom, Danny," he said, pointing to a corner of the shop. "I'll sweep the coffin out and lean it on its end, like it did have dirt and mud inside."

"Where can I hide when somebody comes?"

Davis looked at Danny and replied with his biggest belly laugh since he left Fort Davis.

"You won't believe this, son, but I already thought of that. I knew you'd be here sooner or later. And since it was you, I should have known it would be sooner!"

"It's good to see you happy," Danny said.

"It is good to see you alive," Davis said. "Now, follow me."

He led Danny across the shop to a long carpenter's table. "This is where I do most of my sawing," he said. "Notice anything different?"

Danny shook his head and waited.

"Look under the table, at the back wall." Danny knelt to the floor and scooted under the table. He pulled aside a blanket, and before him stood a small round room made of stones.

"What is this, Jim Davis?"

"It's your home away from home, Danny. It used to be a fireplace. But I talked the officers out of a wood-burning stove, and I just covered up the fireplace. Waiting for you."

"You know what I like most about it?" Danny asked.

"Let me guess. It's made out of stone so snakes can't get you?"

Danny shuddered to think of the rattle-snakes. "No," he said. "I don't have to be closed up tight in the dark, like in a coffin. The front wall is a blanket."

"And did you look at the blanket, Danny? It is a Navajo blanket."

"You are a good man, Jim Davis."

Davis smiled and patted Danny on the shoulder. "Let me boil some water for coffee, and you can tell me how you got here," he said.

For the next hour, Jim Davis and Danny Blackgoat traded stories about their recent adventures. Danny told his friend about the Grady ranch and how kind they were to him.

"They welcomed me like no white people I ever knew, Jim Davis. Almost like I was one of them."

"You are like them in many ways," said Davis. "You are a good, hardworking young man, and Mr. Grady saw that in you."

When he told Davis about Manny and the slave traders, Davis bit his lip and clenched his fists. "You are lucky to be alive. You know that, don't you?"

"Yes," Danny said. "I am alive for my family, to help them just like I helped the Gradys." When he finished his stories, Danny took a long sip of coffee, letting Jim Davis know he was ready to listen.

"Danny, I wish you could have seen all the excitement you caused when they discovered you were not in your bed that morning!" he began.

"Did they know I was buried in the graveyard?"

"No, I covered up the grave after you rode away. But that didn't stop the soldiers from suspecting me. I think they still do. If they find you here, Danny, we could both hang. And since the soldiers saw you at the Gradys' a few days ago, they'll be looking for you here. And you know the first place they'll look?"

"They will look for me to be with my family," Danny said.

"Yes," said Davis, "and then they'll look for you here."

As if on cue, a loud knocking sound shook the front door.

"Open this door!" a voice shouted. "Now!"

Davis pointed to the fireplace and Danny jumped to his feet. He leapt under the table and was about to close the blanket over his hideout when he spotted his coffee cup. The pounding grew so strong the door rattled on its hinges.

"Open this door now, or we'll blow it open!"

Danny crawled from the fireplace to retrieve his cup, while Davis made his way to the door. Just before he opened it, Davis glanced over his shoulder. He frantically waved to Danny to hide himself. Danny did, leaving his half-filled coffee cup on the floor for all to see.

Chapter 11
The Shadow

Jim Davis lifted the latch of his door and slowly opened it. Six soldiers, five infantrymen and a corporal, stood before him. The corporal's hand gripped a sword hanging at his side, and his men held their rifles in front of them, ready to fire if needed.

"Why was your door locked?" the corporal asked. "This door is not supposed to have a lock on it."

"I keep it locked 'cause of the slave traders," Davis said. "I'm too old to be fighting that gang of killers."

"Carpenter, what is your name?" asked the corporal, as his men lowered their rifles.

"Jim Davis, and I'm pleased to meet you," Davis said, extending his hand.

"I am Corporal Doyle," the soldier said, ignoring Davis's outstretched hand. "And before you were captured you were a rebel soldier, am I correct?"

"Yes, sir," said Davis.

"You were fighting to protect slave traders," said the corporal.

Davis hung his head and said nothing in reply.

"You know the slave traders could never enter this fort. They would never try. Their prey sleeps and lives outside the fort."

"Prey?" said Davis, lifting his eyes to face the corporal. "You mean the Navajo people, struggling to stay alive?"

"We live in a savage world, Jim Davis. And if you want to live another day, protected by the United States Army, you play by our rules. Do you understand?"

"Yes," Davis replied.

Corporal Doyle turned to his men. "Tear the lock off that door, and let's move on." Two soldiers grabbed a metal bar and pried the latch from the wall and the door. "Keep the lock," he said, staring at Davis. "We might need it later, to lock this rebel inside his shop."

From his new hiding spot in the stone fireplace, Danny Blackgoat had a frightening thought. *With no lock on the door, anybody can come in whenever they want, day or night.*

"Drop by anytime," Davis said, waving as he closed the door.

With the soldiers gone, he walked slowly to his worktable and sat on the bench. "Stay where you are for a while," he said quietly. Danny reached under the blanket and tapped Davis's boot, letting him know he understood.

"I have a question for you," a voice said, floating through the room. Davis turned to see the corporal, standing in the doorway. He had never even heard the door open.

"Sorry, I didn't hear you," said Davis. "I was just getting back to work."

The corporal pointed to the coffee cups on the floor. "There are two cups. Did you have a visitor this morning?"

"Yes, I did," Davis said. "The men who pick up the coffins. I always have coffee ready for anybody who stops by. Would you like a cup? It'll just take me a minute." Davis hurried to the stove and lifted the pan for boiling water.

"Oh no," he said. "Looks like I'm out of water."

"I did not come by for coffee," the corporal said. "I came by to let you know we have our eyes on you. We know you were a friend of that Indian boy, the one who escaped from Fort Davis. He stole a horse, and he will hang. So be warned, unless you want to join him."

"Sir, we had our falling out long ago. I was glad to see him go."

"I am no friend of savages or rebels," the corporal said, slamming the door closed.

Davis stood as still as a statue for a long moment. *If the corporal asks the graveyard workers about morning coffee, I am in trouble*, he thought. He took a deep breath and hung his head. He wanted to talk to Danny, to come up with a new plan. But even a simple conversation was dangerous—with no lock on the door.

He returned to his bench without speaking. Danny knew to be very quiet till the immediate danger had passed. Half an hour later, Davis stepped outside, looking up and down the street. Dozens of soldiers were following orders and performing their duties, and none of their duties seemed to involve Jim Davis.

After sundown Davis cooked corn stew on his small stove. He lit his oil lamp, keeping the flame low, and the room was darker than usual. When the stew was ready, he handed a cup to Danny under the blanket. When Danny didn't take the stew, Davis knelt under the table and whispered, "It's safe now, Danny. Here, I made us some stew."

No answer.

"Danny, we're alone now. You have to eat."

Still no answer.

Davis flung back the blanket and crawled closer, peering into the fireplace opening. In the darkness he saw only shadows. "Danny, are you there?"

He reached into the fireplace and felt the cold stones. Shaking his head and wondering what was happening, Davis felt a tapping on his shoulder.

"Hey!" he hollered, banging his head on the table. He rolled to his back and saw the outline of someone standing over him.

Davis scrambled to his feet. "You could have let me know you were here," he said. He squinted his eyes, still unable to see in the dim light. He guessed a soldier was standing before him.

"Can I help you?"

The shadow answered, "Yes," nodding his head.

Davis stood trembling before this nighttime intruder.

"Who are you?" he asked.

"I am not supposed to talk," the shadow whispered, and in the light of a thin moonbeam, Jim Davis saw his friend, Danny Blackgoat.

Chapter 12
Invisible Navajo

"I am sorry, Jim Davis, but if I was always where people expect me to be, I would not be alive today."

"I know, Danny, but you need to remember— I'm the man who had the heart attack. You can't do that to me, ever again."

"Even if you sneak up behind me while I am praying?" Danny asked.

In spite of himself, Davis laughed. "All right, but if you recall, I did allow you to finish," he said, gripping Danny's hand in a strong handshake. "Friends again?"

"Yes, but I can't stay here anymore, not even tonight," Danny said.

"You're right," Davis agreed. "Chances are good the soldiers will come looking for you here tomorrow, and they'll tear this place apart. I need to uncover the fireplace and maybe move the table, so it doesn't look like I'm trying to hide anything."

"I need to leave the fort and get to my family. Can Rick help?"

"Maybe, but they'll be watching him too," Davis said.

In the silence that followed, a soft knock sounded at the door.

Davis looked at Danny and Danny froze, but for only a moment. In a flash he leapt behind a stack of boards against the wall. Davis waited, hoping whoever was knocking would think he was asleep and leave.

Whup, whup, whup. Once more the knock floated across the carpentry shop, like a soft cloud. "Just a minute," Davis said. "I was nodding off to sleep."

He opened the door, expecting a group of soldiers. Instead, a young girl stood before him, staring at the ground at her feet. "Are you Rick's daughter?" Davis asked.

The girl nodded, and Davis reached for her shoulder and hurried her inside. He looked right and left, peering into the shadows, looking for any movement or dark shapes that should not be there. When he saw nothing, he entered his shop and turned to the girl.

"Did anyone see you? Did the soldiers follow you? Are you sure?"

"No one saw me," she answered. "I was very careful. My mother and father do not even know I am here."

"Where do they think you are?"

"Asleep under my blanket."

"Oh my," said Davis. "I hope they don't discover you're gone. Rick has seen how cruel the slave traders can be. He'll look everywhere for you."

"I won't stay long," she said. "I want to make sure Danny Blackgoat is safe. Do you know where he is?"

Davis hesitated. *Rick's daughter thinks it is safe to come to my shop in the middle of the night,* he thought. *If she knows Danny is here, she won't leave until she sees him. We'll all be in danger.*

"You can trust me," the girl said, as if reading his thoughts. "I will tell no one except my mother and father, and they know to be careful."

Davis smiled. "You are as smart as Danny," he said. "What is your name?"

"I am Jane," she said. "My grandmother's clan is Bead People, and my grandfather's is Bitter Water. We live at Fort Davis but came to Fort Sumner with my father on one of his trips."

"My name is Jim Davis, and I am of the Davis family from Virginia. Before I tell you where Danny is, let me have one more look around." Davis rose and walked to a single window, covered only by wooden shutters, at the rear wall of the shop. He opened the shutters and looked up and down the roadway. Seeing nothing unusual, he crossed the shop and quietly creaked open the front door.

"Looks like we are safe for now," he said to Jane. "Why did you come here looking for Danny?"

"I heard soldiers talking to my father, asking him to keep a lookout for Danny. You are his best friend. You helped him escape. He will come to you as soon as he can."

"You are right," Davis said. "He is here now. Danny," he whisper-called across the shop. "It's safe to come out."

From behind the stack of boards, Danny stepped forward. He hung his head and mumbled, "It is good to see you, Jane."

Davis smiled and shook his head. "Danny Blackgoat," he said. "I have never seen you so shy." When Danny said nothing, he realized the two Navajos were more than friends. "I'm gonna guard the door for a few minutes," he said, leaving Danny and Jane alone. In a short while, Jane joined him at the door.

"I better go," Jane said. "And do not worry. I will walk in the shadows, and if anyone sees me, I will tell them I am lost."

"It is nice to meet you, Jane. I guess Danny told you he will not be here in the morning."

"Yes," Jane said. "I know I will see him again. He always surprises me."

"Danny Blackgoat is full of surprises," Davis said with a smile. As they turned to look at him, Danny crawled through the open window and leapt to the ground, disappearing into the night.

Davis smiled at the truth of his words. "Jane," he said, "maybe you can stop by often, during the day. Just for a short visit. That way if you really need to let me know something, or if I have news your family should hear, the soldiers will already think of us as friends. Your coming here will not seem unusual."

"Yes, I will do that," Jane said. "Good-bye for now."

Davis closed the door quietly behind her, then walked to the rear of the carpentry shop to close the window shutters. "I've got a Navajo boy climbing out my window, a Navajo girl hiding in the shadows around my front door, it's the middle of the night, and the soldiers want to hang me. How did I ever get myself into this mess?"

He stood for a moment and thought of the evening.

Would I do it all again? he asked himself. *Yes, I would. These Navajos are a good people, and I'll help them any way I can.*

He climbed into bed with a smile on his face, and before he drifted off to sleep, he said a quiet prayer. "May Jane return safely to her family, and may Danny Blackgoat leave the fort before the soldiers find him."

Only one of his prayers was answered.

Chapter 13
Soldiers in the Shadows

Jane arrived at her family's campsite to hear her father snoring and rolling out of his blanket.

"What was that noise!" he shouted. Jane hurried to his side, pretending he had awakened her.

"Nothing, Dad. You must have been having a bad dream. I didn't hear any noise."

"Oh, I am sorry, Jane. I didn't mean to wake you up."

Soon Jane and her family were asleep again, but Danny Blackgoat never made it to his family.

Throughout the day, the corporal had asked questions of anyone who knew Jim Davis or

Rick. The gravediggers told him of the coffin Davis had removed that day.

"Jim Davis claimed that empty coffin was filled with mud, and that's what made it so heavy," said the sergeant. "But he was very careful not to let us look in the coffin."

"And he sure did close the door to his shop in a hurry," added the private.

"I spoke to some soldiers who just arrived from Fort Davis, where Jim Davis was a prisoner before he came here," the corporal said. "They claimed they saw this Indian boy and shot at him before he got away. They said he might be coming here, where his family lives."

Like a mosquito buzzing around in the dark, the corporal could not get Danny Blackgoat out of his mind. "He stole a horse from the United States Army, and he must pay for it," he said to himself over and over again. When the corporal had entered the carpentry shop and surprised Davis, he saw no one else in the shop.

But there were two coffee cups! he thought.

As the sun sank beneath the low-lying hills to the west, the corporal had his usual evening meal with the men serving under him. He then returned to his barracks for a quiet evening of poker playing with the other officers.

After losing two quick hands of poker, he slapped his cards to the table and rose to go. "I have some business to attend to that will not wait," he told his fellow officers.

"Anything we can help you with?" asked a lieutenant.

"No, it's about a young Indian runaway. I think I'll take care of this myself."

He left the barracks with his long-range rifle over his shoulder, loaded and ready to fire, and his pistol at his side. *If I were that boy, I'd want to be with my family*, he thought to himself. *But he can't go there till after dark. I think the gravediggers were right. He is with Jim Davis, hiding somewhere in his carpentry shop. But he won't stay there, not tonight. He knows we'll be looking for him in the morning. He's not safe anywhere in the fort. That Navajo boy will try to escape from the fort tonight!*

On his way to the carpentry shop, the corporal stopped by the enlisted men's barracks, where they had their own poker game going.

"You two," he said to the best marksmen. "Sergeant Tolar and Sergeant Chester, come with me. Bring your rifles, pistols, and plenty of ammunition."

"What is it, sir?" asked a young soldier, newly arrived at the fort. "Is there an attack on the fort?" The other soldiers smiled at his inexperience, knowing they would be alerted with the sound of bugles during an attack.

"No, at ease, men," the corporal said. "The man we are hunting is unarmed, but he is Indian, and we will shoot him if he runs. Is that understood?" he asked.

"Yes, sir!" they both replied.

"Good. Let's go now."

They hurried after the corporal, moving from the barracks to the stables where the horses were kept and fed. As they neared the carpentry shop, the corporal held up his hand, and the men stopped.

"The carpenter is a rebel prisoner who arrived from Fort Davis a few days ago. I think the Indian boy is hiding out with him. We want to capture the boy first, but if we can't, we will shoot him. He stole a horse, and I want him to hang, for the other thieving Indians to see. A body hanging over the campsite, swinging back and forth as the buzzards feast on his bones, that would be a message hard to ignore."

The marksmen nodded.

Out of habit the men approached the door to the carpentry shop, but the corporal stopped them with a wave of his arm. "There is a rear window to the shop," he whispered. "I want both of you to circle the building. Stay in the shadows. And remember, we want this boy alive. If you have to shoot him, shoot to wound, not to kill."

The soldiers dashed around the corner, anxious to do what they were trained to do best. The corporal gave them a few minutes, then stepped to the door. He took a deep breath before knocking.

"Let us see what secrets you have for us now, you rebel traitor," he said to himself. He never knocked on the door. *Pow!* A gun blast sounded from the rear of the building, then another. *Pow!*

The corporal flung the door open and ran across the shop to the rear window. Jim Davis had opened the curtains and was peering into the dark night.

"What is it?" Davis called out. He was about to call Danny by name when the corporal entered the building.

"Out of the way!" shouted the corporal, shoving Davis to the floor. "Did you hit him?" he called to his men.

Pow! Pow! came the reply.

Chapter 14
Navajo Blood

Danny leapt to the ground but knew right away he was not alone. A strong hand, a soldier's hand, reached out and grabbed his arm. He shook himself free and ran with the speed of a deer to the wall.

"He's over here!" the soldier shouted. "I almost had him."

Danny rolled to the ground just in time, as a rifle blast flew over his head. He spotted two soldiers coming in his direction. The guards in the tower came to life, shouting, "Who's firing the guns?"

"Army marksmen here, after a Navajo boy! See if you can find him!"

Two guards carrying lanterns hurried down from the tower and joined the soldiers. Danny saw no trees or bushes to hide behind, nothing but open space between him and the wall, as guards with lanterns searched the grounds for him.

If they see me, they will shoot me, Danny thought.

Corporal Doyle gripped the ledge of the window and lifted himself to the ground. In the moonlight he saw the marksmen running to the wall of the fort. *There is no way that boy can escape now*, he thought. *The guards watch the walls night and day, and he'll never make it through the gate.* The corporal joined his men at the wall.

"You won't believe this," Sergeant Tolar said, pointing to a pile of bloody stones scattered near the wall. Kicking the stones aside, the corporal saw a small hole beneath the wooden boards and blood still dripping from the bottom of the boards.

"Barely big enough for a dog," said Sergeant Tolar.

"Big enough for a skinny Navajo boy," said Corporal Doyle.

The corporal spit on the ground and cursed.

"What did you find?" came a voice from the tower. The bouncing light of a lantern approached the men, and a guard soon joined them.

"Looks like somebody dug an escape hole," said Corporal Doyle, pointing to the blood-soaked stones.

"I don't know how that could happen," the guard replied. "We watch this wall night and day, from the tower and by foot patrol." He shook his head and cast a nervous glance at the corporal.

"Well, somebody's not doing their job," the corporal said. "We will get to the bottom of this oversight in the morning. Right now we have a prisoner to catch. He's leaving a bloody trail wherever he goes. He shouldn't be hard to find."

The marksmen stood at attention and waited for orders.

"Sergeant Tolar, go back to the barracks and let the officers know we need ten horsemen, with their rifles loaded, at the gates of the fort as soon as possible. "Yes, sir," said Sergeant Tolar, saluting and hurrying away.

"You," he said to the guard, "get me two men with lanterns. Now!"

Before leaving the site, Corporal Doyle knelt to the ground and picked up a stone. He touched his finger to a crimson glob of blood, shining in the lantern light. "Your blood is still wet on the stone," he whispered to himself. "You cannot be far away." He stuck the stone in his pocket and rose to his feet.

When the men with the lanterns appeared, he said, "We have a wounded Indian boy who escaped through a hole beneath the wall. We don't know how bad he is hurt. He might be running away. He might be dying in the rocks nearby. If he is alive, capture him but do not kill him."

"Yes, sir," the men shouted.

"We want to make as much noise as possible. We want these Indians to be afraid, so no one will help the boy. Understood?"

They nodded, and the corporal whispered, leaning close with a mean stare in his eyes, "Now, fire your rifles over their heads and let us spread the fear!"

The soldiers lowered their lanterns and aimed at the sky.

"Fire!" shouted the corporal.

Pow! Pow! Pow!

The midnight moon shone down on the camps of sleeping Navajo families. Hearing the gunshots, men jumped to their feet. Children cried, infants screamed, and women pulled their children close. Corporal Doyle smiled at the sounds of fear—moving across the night like waves of sand in a desert storm.

"We will find you," he said, "and you will wish you had stayed at Fort Davis. A rattlesnake bite will seem like a blessing when I finish with you."

Doyle and his men exited the gate and moved through the Navajo families. They passed through hundreds of camps, where men and women wrapped their children in blankets and covered them from even the sight of the soldiers.

The corporal kicked the smoking remains of campfires, asking, "Did any of you see a wounded Navajo boy running from the fort?"

Many of the Navajos turned away, unable to understand his words. Even those who spoke English wanted nothing to do with this nightmare and said nothing in reply. But many knew of Danny Blackgoat. They knew of his escape, they knew he was nearby, and they would help him any way they could.

"If anything looks suspicious, yank away the blankets!" shouted Doyle. "Take no chances."

But he gave this order too late. Danny Blackgoat was close to the fort, and the soldiers had already passed him by. He lay in a blanket held by a young woman, a family friend from Canyon De Chelly. His own grandfather had found Danny, fallen and bleeding on the ground, soon after he crawled under the stone escape hole.

"How did you know I would be here, Grandfather?" Danny had asked him.

"My grandson, as soon as I heard the rifles, I knew where to find you. I dug the hole months ago, for no reason, just a vision that someday it might save your life. I was right, wasn't I?" his grandfather said, smiling.

"Thank you, Grandfather," Danny said, holding his thigh, just above his knee, where the bullet had hit him and flown through his flesh.

"I knew you would never rest until you entered the fort. I knew that when you were in danger and the soldiers were chasing you, you would spot the stones at the base of the wall. I knew you would think 'Why are those stones here? They hide something.' I knew you would dig and find the hole."

His grandfather rocked back and forth, holding Danny as if he were an infant.

"Jane has been visiting with us for some time now," he continued. "She comes early in the morning, before the soldiers are on the lookout for anyone leaving the fort. She started a routine, so no one would suspect her of anything. She is, after all, the daughter of a white man who drives a wagon for the soldiers.

"Jane has a bucket and gathers water for her family almost every morning. She visits us, bringing us any news of you, Danny."

Danny nodded, in too much pain to speak.

"Now," said his grandfather, "we should be very quiet. I cannot move you till the soldiers return to the fort." The elder Navajo reached into a leather bag and pulled out a handful of ground corn. Holding Danny close to his chest, he reached for his wounded leg.

The husband of the young woman helped Danny's grandfather remove the blood-soaked trousers. After making certain the bullet had passed through Danny's flesh, his grandfather stuffed the wound with the ground corn to stop the bleeding. But the bullet had sliced a deep hole in Danny's leg, and the bleeding did not stop.

His grandfather took another handful of ground corn and rubbed it into the bullet hole. Danny winced in pain, and his grandfather placed his palm on Danny's forehead.

"You will live, Danny Blackgoat. This I know."

Hearing the calming words of his grandfather, his teacher, Danny relaxed and the pain fell away. The soldiers continued shooting their rifles into the sky, terrifying the Navajo children and angering the adults.

An hour before sunrise, as the sky offered a hint of the coming morning, Sergeant Tolar returned to the stone tunnel. Thinking he spotted a trail of blood, he knelt to the ground.

"Corporal Doyle," he shouted, jumping to his feet. "He left a bloody trail! We can find him, over here!"

Soon he was joined by the corporal and several soldiers on horseback. The corporal carried a lantern. "Cavalrymen," he said, "follow the trail till you find him. He can't escape now, and if you find anyone helping the boy, bring them in as well. They are as guilty as he is for helping a horse thief escape."

He turned to Sergeant Tolar and handed him the lantern. "The hillside is rocky. You'll have no trouble staying up with the horsemen," he said. "Lead the way with the lantern and keep your eyes and ears close to the ground."

The men saluted a reply and turned their horses to the hillside, where splatters of blood sketched an easy path to follow.

Chapter 15
The Bloody Trail

The men eased their horses up the steep hillside as Sergeant Tolar held the lantern close to the ground. The trail was easy to follow.

"He's been hit good," the sergeant said. "Lotta blood leaving that boy. He'll be lucky to make it till morning."

"The corporal wants him alive," said a cavalryman, "so let's try to make him happy."

Halfway up the hillside, the bloody trail took a downturn. "He knows he's too weak to climb the hill. We'll find him in that camp," Sergeant Tolar said, pointing to a gathering of Navajo families camped nearby.

The blood grew thicker now, easier to follow. Soon the soldiers burst upon an old Navajo man and a young husband and wife. The wife clung to a blanket, holding someone inside.

"You better hope that boy is not the wounded one we're looking for," Tolar said, certain he had found Danny. He grabbed the blanket and the men lifted their shotguns to their shoulders, ready to fire if they were threatened.

"What are you doing?" the Navajo husband asked, standing to protect his wife. A soldier leapt from his horse and hit him in the jaw with the butt of his rifle.

"No," said the woman, clutching the blanket with both hands.

Tolar flung the blanket aside. Instead of Danny, he saw a pair of young Navajo children, wrapping their arms around their mother and hiding their eyes from the glaring light of the lantern. "Where is the boy?" shouted Tolar.

"These are my daughters," the woman said. "I have no sons. Please leave us alone."

"Where is the boy, the wounded boy?" said Tolar. "We followed a trail of his blood to your camp!"

"I found a blanket," said the elder Navajo man. "Here. I found it on the hillside and carried it here. We don't have enough blankets, and it is freezing cold. My daughter could clean the blood from it."

"Did you see a boy when you found the blanket?" Tolar asked.

"No, it was very dark. I saw nobody."

"Get up, old man, and show us where you found the blanket!" he shouted, losing his patience. The elder hesitated.

"You said you followed a trail of blood," he said, staring at the ground. "Where the blood begins, that's where I found the blanket." Tolar gave him a long, hard stare before turning to his men.

"The boy's not here!" he shouted, jerking his horse's reins. "Get the blanket, and let's return to the fort. Corporal Doyle will be furious, but we can't do anything about that now."

When the soldiers were well out of earshot, Danny's grandfather lifted his head from behind a boulder, ten feet from where the woman lay with her two infant daughters. He looked left and right, making certain no soldiers were near.

"Thank you," he whispered. "You saved my grandson's life."

"He is a good boy," said the elder, "and we are glad to help him. But my granddaughters— my daughter too—have his blood from the gunshot wound. Can you make them clean?"

"Yes," said Danny's grandfather. "After the morning prayer, I will return to camp and let Danny's mother and father know he is safe. I will return with water for the cleansing."

Sergeant Tolar led the soldiers down the rocky path to the gates of the fort, where Corporal Doyle waited. "Did you find him?" asked the corporal, looking eagerly at the returning soldiers. "Is he still alive?"

"We thought we had him," said Tolar, "but this is all we found." He told the story of tracing the bloody trail of the blanket, only to find it wrapped around two Navajo infants.

As Corporal Doyle led his men through the gates of Fort Sumner, he was met by a dozen officers on horseback. They were lined up on either side of the road and dressed in full military regalia. A soldier lifted a trumpet to his mouth and blew the first loud notes of a military march, but Doyle waved his hands and signaled for him to stop. He lowered his trumpet, and a half-blown note withered and died in the dark.

"We are here to honor you for capturing the horse thief," said Major Henson, a well-respected leader of the US Cavalry. He leaned forward and saluted Doyle. "We heard your men shot and captured him. We are ready for his trial and hanging. Is he still alive?"

"Here is all we found of the boy," Doyle said, tossing the blanket at the foot of the major's horse. The major stared at the blood-covered blanket.

"We heard the shots," said Major Henson. "There was a report that the boy was being captured. Is this even the same boy who stole the horse?"

"I have no doubt it is the same boy."

"And how do you know this?"

"We found him escaping from the carpentry shop of his friend from Fort Davis."

The major took a long, deep breath, unaccustomed and uncomfortable with being embarrassed. "So, where is this horse-thieving Indian boy?" he asked.

"Your guess is as good as mine," replied Corporal Doyle, gesturing over his shoulder. Feeling the harsh glare of the major, he added, "I am sorry, sir. I meant no disrespect. I am disgusted with my own conduct, and I have not slept in almost thirty hours."

"I accept your apology," said the major. "Have we arrested this carpenter yet?"

"No, sir, we have not."

"And why not?"

"I had hoped to catch him with the boy. We circled the carpentry shop last night. That's how we found the boy. He crawled through a window of the shop and was running away when my men shot him."

"And you could not capture a wounded Indian boy?" asked Major Henson. He turned to his fellow officers. "We will have no celebration today. No hanging either, it appears. Return to your quarters and change uniforms. We have a workday ahead of us."

"Major Henson," said Doyle. "I want to arrest that carpenter, Davis. He is a rebel soldier, and he is just as guilty as the savage. Both of them should hang."

"Of course we will arrest Jim Davis," said the major. "That should have happened a long time ago. I will find some trustworthy men and arrest him this morning. Would you like to come along?"

He turned away without waiting for a reply.

Chapter 16
Death by Hanging
or Firing Squad?

An hour before sunrise, Major Henson and a dozen soldiers entered the carpentry shop. They found Jim Davis slumped over his worktable and snoring loudly. Major Henson approached him and pounded his fists on the table.

"Hey, what are you doing?" asked Davis, startled from a dark dream of Danny Blackgoat climbing a canyon wall, chased by rattlesnakes.

"We are here to do what should have been done long ago," replied the major. "Hands behind your back, Jim Davis. You are under military arrest. Men, tie him up!"

The soldiers lifted Davis from his workbench and jerked his arms backward, tying his wrists with a tight rope.

"What did I do?" Davis asked.

"You know what you did," said Major Henson. "You helped that Indian boy escape. He's a horse thief, and I'm thinking that makes you one too."

Davis said nothing, but a tide of joy swept over him. *If I helped that Indian boy escape, Danny Blackgoat is alive!* he thought. He hung his head to hide his smile.

"Where are you taking me?" Davis asked.

"That's one too many questions," the major said, nodding to a soldier. Knowing what the major wanted, the soldier struck Davis in the jaw with the butt of his rifle. He slumped forward, stunned by the blow, and his head swayed from side to side.

"Any more questions?" asked the major. "Take him to headquarters," he said, turning to his men. They pushed Davis forward, and he stumbled through the door and into the darkness. The gravediggers arrived, ready for their morning work. They pulled their wagon to a halt as the soldiers left the carpentry shop. They were shocked to see Jim Davis, his face already swollen and blue from the bruises, tied and being dragged away by Major Henson's men.

"I wouldn't want to be in his shoes," said one.

"Where they're taking him, he won't need any shoes," said the other.

The sun peeked over the nearby mountains, casting a warm glow on Danny and his grandfather. At that moment, Jim Davis sat on a bench awaiting trial for horse theft and helping a prisoner escape. The only issue to be settled in the trial of a rebel soldier, Davis realized, was whether he would die by hanging or firing squad.

A lone soldier stood guard over Davis while the officers had their morning breakfast. He was staring out the window at the noose on the scaffolding in the distance, hoping for a hanging rather than a firing squad. He heard the door close quietly behind him and jumped to attention.

Jane stood by the door. "I did not mean to startle you," she said. "I went by the carpentry shop to see my friend, and they told me he was gone. They said he was arrested. What did he do? He's always been nice to me."

"Young lady, you better leave here right away," the soldier said. "Major Henson is likely to arrest anybody who's a friend of this rebel. He's gonna hang today or die by firing squad."

"I'm going. Thank you," said Jane, turning to the door. She reached for the doorknob, then paused and asked again, "What did he do?"

"They say he stole a horse and helped an Indian boy escape. The boy was shot last night, but he got away."

"If he got away, how do they know he was shot?" she asked.

The soldier tilted his head and pursed his lips before replying. "You sure ask a lot of questions, young lady. But if you need evidence, there it is," he said, pointing to a blanket folded up neatly on the floor. The Navajo blanket, of green and yellow sheep's wool, was covered with patches of dried blood.

Without replying, Jane walked quickly from the building, holding back her tears. She ran to their campsite, where they were holding breakfast, awaiting her return.

"What did you find out?" asked Rick, her father.

"Jim Davis has been arrested," Jane said. "They did not catch Danny. They shot him, but he got away."

"Are you sure he was shot?"

"I saw the blanket with his blood all over it," she said, sobbing as she spoke. "He might be dying now, somewhere in the mountains."

Chapter 17
Confederate Soldier's Trial

Following a cheerful breakfast filled with stories of "that troublemaking Indian boy," Major Henson stood and announced, "It's time we bring the rebel to justice." He lifted his cup and chugged down the last of his morning coffee, then whispered aloud for all to hear, "Coffee now, whiskey tonight, to celebrate the hanging of a rebel traitor!"

Accompanied by Corporal Doyle and the two marksmen, Major Henson marched to the headquarters, where Davis waited. He flung open the door and ordered the guard, "Keep everyone away till we finish this matter. Stand outside and let no one enter."

"Yes, sir," the guard said, saluting and leaving the officers alone with Jim Davis. Davis sat with his hands tied behind him, head down, and glanced up at the officers. He did not know the major, but he knew Corporal Doyle wanted him dead.

"Let us get started," said Major Henson. "Corporal Doyle, there is paper and ink at my desk. Take notes as you witness the proceedings, and I will use them in making my report."

Doyle moved to the desk and began.

"Now," said the major, turning to Davis. "You hid this young boy. What is his name?"

"Danny Blackgoat," said Davis.

"Yes. You hid this boy in your carpentry shop, is that correct?"

Davis turned his head away without speaking.

"Before we go any further, Mr. Davis, let me remind you that you are a traitor in the eyes of the United States Army, a Confederate rebel who lifted arms against your own nation. We could hang you today for that reason alone. But we want the truth. And," he said, leaning so close that Davis smelled his breath, "we will get it."

He gripped Davis's swollen jaw till Davis winced from the pain.

"You hid the boy here. He escaped from Fort Davis, and you hid him in your shop."

"He showed up at my door last night, and I let him in," Davis said. "He was hungry, and I fed him."

"You did not report a runaway prisoner. And you knew he was a runaway. You were his friend at Fort Davis."

"I saved his life when a prisoner put a rattlesnake in his bed," Davis said, lifting his head to face the major. "I cut his leg and drained the poison, the snake venom."

Major Henson stepped back in surprise. He knew none of the details of Danny Blackgoat's troubles. Henson paused for a moment, but it was an important moment. Jim Davis saw a slice of sympathy in the eyes of the major.

"He should have let the savage die!" shouted Corporal Doyle. "Instead he helped him escape."

Major Henson looked back and forth at the two men. He saw hatred in the face of one, and a paternal caring in the eyes of the other.

"Is this true?" he finally asked Davis.

"I didn't see the boy for almost a month before he escaped," Davis said, truthfully. "He made me mad, and I stopped speaking to him," he added, quite untruthfully.

"I did not ask if you spoke to him," Major Henson said. "I asked if you helped him escape." Davis turned his face and fell silent.

"So maybe you did not help him escape. Maybe he stole the horse and escaped on his own. You do know a horse was missing from the fort the day of his escape?" the major said, reaching for his jaw.

"Okay, yes, I knew a horse was missing."

"This Navajo boy stole the horse on his own?" said the major in a low, mean whisper. "You know that when we capture him, he will hang for stealing the horse. And he is badly wounded, about to bleed to death. We will capture him."

"I will tell you the truth, Major," Jim Davis said, in a clear, strong voice. "And take good notes on what I am about to say, Corporal Doyle. I stole the horse. I stole it from Fort Davis and gave it to the young Navajo man, Danny Blackgoat. He never asked where the horse came from. He never knew it was stolen."

When he finished his confession, Davis breathed hard and slumped over in his chair. He fought against the full knowledge of what he had just done—of what would happen to him now.

"You are telling us that the boy you call Danny Blackgoat did not steal the horse?" the corporal asked, leaning close to Jim Davis and shaking his head in disbelief.

"I took the horse from the stables at Fort Davis and gave it to him," said Davis. "He did not know where the horse came from."

"You are admitting to being a horse thief?"

"If taking a horse to keep a young man alive makes me a horse thief, then that is what I am."

"We are not interested in why you stole the horse, Mr. Davis," Major Henson said. "In truth, we are not interested in anything you have to say. We are only having this hearing for military records, so your execution can clearly be shown as the punishment for crimes you have committed. Let me read your notes, Corporal Doyle."

Major Henson spoke to Doyle and began reading the notes and discussing changes. Davis hung his head in silence. Exhausted and weary from the last two days, he closed his eyes and floated away. He imagined Danny lying in the mountains and struggling to stay alive.

Over time, Davis had come think of Danny Blackgoat as his son. *By my confession I am saving my son's life*, he repeated to himself over and over. *I am saving my son's life. I could not save my first son, but I will save this one.*

His mind shifted through the years to the battlegrounds of the Civil War, where he and his son served in the army of the South under General Robert E. Lee. They fought together as Lee's army invaded Pennsylvania in 1863. On the final day of the Battle of Gettysburg, as Jim Davis was captured and dragged away, he saw an explosion of cannonballs on Cemetery

Ridge. He later learned he had seen his own son's death from a distance.

I could not save my first son from the war and the cannons, but I can save this Navajo boy. He is my second son, and I will see that he lives.

With a firm-set, swollen jaw, Jim Davis lifted his head to face whatever the day brought down upon him. He was startled from his thoughts to the present by the voice of Major Henson.

"You have just confessed to horse theft, Jim Davis. As you know, the penalty is death by hanging." He turned to the marksmen, who stood by the door with their rifles at their sides. "You, let the officers know we should prepare for a hanging at noon today. Find a wagon and driver and be swift. This affair is almost over."

The affair was far from over. Rick soon heard the news of Jim Davis admitting to stealing the horse. The gravediggers passed his barracks and stopped to spread the latest news.

"Did you hear? That carpenter who made the coffins, that Jim Davis fellow, he's been hiding a Navajo runaway. And he stole a horse too, that's what they're saying."

Rick knew what he had to do. He loaded his wagon with supplies for Fort Davis, a day earlier than expected. "Susan," he said to his wife, "Danny Blackgoat needs to know that Jim Davis is risking his life for him. I'm going to find him."

"Please don't put yourself in danger," she said.

"We are already in danger," Rick said. "I am not one of them, and they know it."

"What can Danny do?"

"I don't know if he can do anything," Rick said. "But we have to give him a chance."

"You can unload your supply wagon, and that's an order," a voice called out. Rick looked up to see an army marksman riding in his direction. He halted his horse and dismounted.

"I am on my way to Fort Davis," Rick said.

"You can delay your trip till later," said the marksman. "Do you need help unloading?"

"No, I have just started," Rick said. "It won't take me a minute. Why do you need my wagon?"

"We need you and your wagon both," the marksman said. "There's a hanging today at noon, and you will be the driver."

"Who is being hanged?" he asked, trembling already for he knew the answer. He knew the name the marksman would say. He closed his eyes and waited.

"Jim Davis," the marksman said. "He will hang at noon."

And I will be the driver, thought Rick.

Chapter 18
Life-Saving Navajo Horse

"I can take care of my wagon," Rick said to the marksman. "I'll have it cleared out and ready to go. I'll be at the hanging half an hour before noon."

"I'll let Major Henson know," the marksman said. "Do not be late." He tipped his hat to Jane and rode away.

"We cannot let Jim Davis hang," said Susan. "He is a good man. We must help him."

"I don't know what we can do," Rick said. "He admitted to stealing a horse."

"If I had not given you the horse, maybe none of this would have happened."

"You didn't give me the horse," Rick said. "Your father gave it to me, to show how much he appreciated my care for his daughter."

"But it was my idea that you use the horse on your trips, to think always of your Navajo family. And it was my idea for Jim Davis to give the pony to Danny Blackgoat, to help him escape."

As Susan spoke of their Navajo horse, Rick was lifting a heavy trunk from the rear of the wagon. He was suddenly struck by a thought. He dropped the trunk, spilling nails and tools all over the ground.

"Are you all right?" Susan asked.

"Yes," Rick said. "I am fine, better than ever. I have the smartest wife in the world, and she doesn't even know it."

"What are you talking about?" Jane asked, but Rick was not listening. He was on his way to the horse stables.

"I'll tell you later," he called out over his shoulder. He rounded the corner of the barracks and broke into a sprint. His lungs burned and his muscles ached, but he didn't stop till he reached the horse corral. He found Danny Blackgoat's horse just where he had hidden it a few days ago, in a remote corner of the corral where only the untrained and troublesome ponies were kept.

"It's time we take a trip," Rick said, and the horse stomped the ground with his right front hoof, as he always did to welcome him. "Nice to see you too," Rick said. He saddled the horse and popped the reins.

"Let's go," he said, leaning over and patting Fire Eye on the neck.

Fire Eye stomped and whinnied and took off in such a hurry he almost threw Rick to the ground. As they neared the gates to the fort, he slowed Fire Eye to a walk. The guards knew Rick well and waved to him as he approached.

"Where's your wagon?" a guard asked.

"No time for a wagon," Rick shouted as he passed through the gate. "I'll be back before you know it."

Rick urged Fire Eye into a slow trot, and when he thought he was out of sight of the guards, he broke into a run, popping the reins and slapping his horse on the hindquarters.

"Let's go, Fire Eye!" he shouted. "We have lives to save!"

He rode at a full gallop to the rising hills, high above where Danny had found the rattlesnake cave. Turning Fire Eye from the road to the hillside, Rick leaned forward and began a slow climb. He soon topped the hill and spotted the cave. No Danny.

Rick took a long, deep breath and looked to the gathering clouds overhead. He patted Fire Eye on the neck and spoke in a quiet voice.

"Any idea where our friend Danny Blackgoat might be?"

Hearing the name of his young Navajo friend, Fire Eye stomped the ground with his right foot. Without any urging from Rick, Fire Eye stepped down the hill as Danny had taught him, taking short, quick steps. He moved at an angle, zigzagging from right to left, but always headed downhill.

Rick was so surprised he almost jerked the reins and pulled Fire Eye to a halt. But something told him to trust this Navajo horse, and he did. When he realized Fire Eye knew how to ride the hills better than he did, he filled the desert air with warm laughter, hugging his horse's neck.

Fire Eye knew of the rattlesnake cave. As they approached the dark hole beneath a boulder, he lifted his legs high, in a slow and careful change of pace. Rick soon saw why Fire Eye carried him down the hill. A water cup lay in the front entrance of the cave, sparkling in the sunlight. "That's the cup the soldiers use," Rick said. "Why is it here?"

He stepped from the saddle to pick up the cup, but it didn't come easily. The cup was stuck in six inches of thick white mud.

"This is mud from the lake," Rick said aloud, "the mud that poisons our water. Wonder how it got here?" He yanked the cup from the ground and found his answer. Carved on the side were the letters DB.

"Danny Blackgoat, you sly young man. What made you think I would ever find your message? You're hiding out at the lake."

Fire Eye stomped his right hoof and whinnied.

"I guess you're right," Rick said. "If I couldn't find it, you would. All right, if we're gonna rescue Danny, we better be on our way." He glanced to the morning sky and guessed he had maybe an hour before the hanging.

"Let's go, boy! If I'm not there, they'll hang him anyway." Rick flung himself on Fire Eye's back and patted his hindquarters. "Come on now!" he said. Soon they were on the road to the fort, taking the shortest route to the lake.

As they topped the hill overlooking the muddy white waters, Rick tugged the reins and pulled Fire Eye to a halt. He rose in the saddle and looked up and down the wide stretch of rocky land surrounding the lake. "He's got to be here somewhere," Rick whispered. On the far side of the lake, he saw a young Navajo girl carrying a wooden pail and walking to the water.

Fire Eye once again began his descent, stepping at an angle from the hillside to the lake. As they neared the girl, he held his hand high in a gesture of friendship, but the girl never even turned to look at him. "He is with his grandfather on the hill behind me," she said quietly.

Rick nodded, said thank you, and urged Fire Eye up the hill. Behind a thick grove of mesquite trees, he found Danny, resting his head on his grandfather's lap.

"He knew you would find him," Grandfather said.

Danny opened his eyes and leapt to his feet. "Ohhhh," he moaned, limping in a small circle and feeling the pain of his leg wound.

"Careful, Danny," Rick said. "Looks like the gunshot didn't kill you, but you still have some healing to do."

"I wanted you to know that I am alive," Danny said. "Can you let Jim Davis know too? They must be angry with him for hiding me."

Rick paused for a brief moment, then realized the time had come. Danny had to know. "They are more than angry, Danny," he said. "In an hour Jim Davis will hang—for stealing the horse and helping you escape."

Chapter 19
Please Believe Me!

The previous night, as Danny Blackgoat lay on the mountainside, bleeding from a shotgun wound to the leg, the dreams of Miss Sarah Grady took a turn for the worse. From her tiny bed in the pine trees of the Grady ranch, Sarah screamed so loud she woke up every living thing for at least a mile.

"He's shot, they shot him!" she shouted, sitting up in bed.

She screamed again and again, finally stuffing her face in a pillow to stop the screaming. Mrs. Grady ran to her daughter's bedside, stubbing her toe on a tree root.

"Sarah, are you all right?" she asked, squatting and rubbing her foot.

Sarah shook her head violently from side to side as she sobbed.

"What is it? Did you have a bad dream?"

Sarah nodded. "You have to believe me, Mother. You must," Sarah said, grabbing her mother's wrists. "Daddy will not. He thinks I am a silly little girl. But I am a young woman, and you must believe me."

"I will try," Mrs. Grady said, swallowing hard and fearing the worst.

"Danny Blackgoat will die if you do not believe me," Sarah said.

"Danny Blackgoat? Your nightmare was about Danny Blackgoat?"

"Yes, Mother, and it was more than a dream," Sarah said, biting her lip in anger as tears fell down her face. "The soldiers at Fort Sumner shot him. He will bleed to death unless we find him."

"Where is he?"

"He is hiding out in the mountains around the fort," said Sarah. "I saw it all. He was in a carpentry shop, just like before. Jim Davis was hiding him. But the soldiers came and he jumped out the window. That's when they shot him. He ran away bleeding."

"Sarah, I know you care for Danny," said her mother. "We all do. He saved our lives. But you cannot know your dream is real."

"Mother," said Sarah, "do you remember when we first met Danny? He saved our lives. It is time for us to save his."

Mrs. Grady stood and took a deep breath. "I believe you," she said. "I do not know if your father will, but together we can convince him. It's time we took a trip to the fort. All of us."

"I love you, Mother," Sarah shouted, rolling over and hugging her mother's knees so hard her mother almost fell to the ground.

"Now let's see what your father has to say."

To their surprise, Mr. Grady was already dressed and saddling his horse. Mrs. Grady was about to ask him what he was doing, when he held up his hand.

"No time to talk," he said. "You cannot talk me out of this. I heard Sarah scream. I know she had a nightmare. I don't even care what the nightmare was about. I am going to Fort

Sumner, and you can come along or stay behind, I don't care. Danny Blackgoat is in trouble, and I'm not going to let that strong young man die. He saved our lives."

"Can I go too?" Mrs. Grady asked.

"Me too, Dad, please," said Sarah.

Less than half an hour after Sarah awakened from her nightmare, the Grady family was on the road to Fort Sumner. They rode as fast as they dared, stopping only to rest their horses. Sarah held tight to the reins of her horse and replayed the nightmare in her mind as they rode. The sun rose far overhead, nearing the noon hour, as they saw the fort in the distance.

"Will they let you in the fort?" asked Mrs. Grady.

"I'm hoping so," Mr. Grady said. Sarah and her mother looked at each other, and Sarah took off at a gallop.

Chapter 20
Danny's Offering

Hearing the news that Jim Davis was scheduled to hang at noon, Danny stood up slowly, ignoring the pain of his wounded leg. "I will not let that happen," he said.

"I'm not sure you can do anything about it, Danny," said Rick.

"I have to try. Fire Eye can carry us both. Grandfather," he said, "please tell my mother and father I will see them this evening. We will be together."

His grandfather stood and held Danny close to his chest. "Stay strong and be blessed," he whispered in his ear.

"What do you plan to do?" Rick asked Danny before they rode away.

"I will ride through the gates and give myself up. If they want to shoot me again, they will. But I will ask them to listen to me first. I will confess to stealing the horse. I will tell them Jim Davis did not steal the horse. I am the one that should hang if anyone does."

"I have another plan," Rick said.

"Please, let me do this," said Danny. "No more running. I want to face up to everything I have done since the soldiers burned our homes and killed our sheep."

"I will not stop you, Danny," Rick said. "But please, I beg of you, do nothing that will give them a reason to kill you both. Say what is the truth and maybe someone will listen."

He climbed to the saddle and helped Danny to the rear of his horse. "You ready to ride?" he asked.

"I am," said Danny, and Rick patted Fire Eye on the hindquarters. The faithful horse climbed the hillside with the speed of one who understood. As they came to the road leading to the fort, Fire Eye hesitated.

"It's okay, boy," said Rick, leaning over and patting his neck. "We're going through the front door today."

The soldiers spotted Rick and Danny Blackgoat long before they came to the gate. "Halt!" a guard shouted. "Halt or we will fire!"

"It's me, Rick," he said, lifting his arms high and guiding Fire Eye to the gates of the fort.

"We see you," shouted the guard, lifting his rifle barrel over the wall of the guard post. "But who is with you?"

"The escaped Navajo boy, Danny Blackgoat," Rick said. "He has come to turn himself in. Please, let us pass."

The guard lowered his rifle, and two horsemen rode to meet Rick. "We will escort you to the officers' headquarters," one said, staring hard at Danny. "Where did you find him?" he asked.

"Wandering around the mountains," Rick said. "I had heard he was shot and thought I might be able to find him."

"Looks like we might have two hangings today," the guard said. "That rebel traitor, the one who helped him escape, is hanging today at noon."

Rick said nothing in reply as the men rode past Jim Davis's carpentry shop, past the stables, and neared the officers' headquarters. "We can handle him from here," said the guard, stepping from his horse and pulling Danny from Fire Eye.

Danny winced in pain as the guard threw him roughly to the ground. He tried to stand but stumbled and fell. The shotgun wound ripped open, and blood flowed in red streaks down his leg.

"Stand up!" shouted the soldier, unmoved by the puddle of blood.

"I can help," Rick said. "I speak some of the boy's language."

"Tell him he better walk on both legs," said the guard. "We ain't got time to carry a savage, wounded or not."

Danny glanced at Rick, letting him know he understood. He was not to respond to anything the soldiers said. He would pretend to speak only Navajo. That would keep Rick close by.

"Danny," Rick said in Navajo, leaning close to the young man. "Say nothing. I have a plan, and do not let them know you understand a word of English."

Danny nodded and did his best to stand tall, as if that was what Rick told him.

"Good," said the soldier. "Now, bring him inside. He can wait with the rebel till we decide his fate." The soldiers entered the room.

"We found the Indian boy," said the guard. "He's wounded but still alive, well enough to stand trial."

Danny spotted Jim Davis sitting in a corner, his head lowered in sadness. A soldier sat nearby with a gun in his lap. He rose quickly and saluted the guard.

"At ease," said the guard. "Can you locate Major Henson? Let him know we captured the Indian boy. He is ready for trial."

The soldier hesitated. "I was ordered by the major to stand guard over Jim Davis," he said.

The guard walked quietly to the soldier—a private who now stood at attention, as still as a desert cactus. He leaned so close, his hot breath blew on the private as he spoke. He waited a long moment, adding to the tension in the room.

"Are you refusing a direct order from a superior?" he asked. "Do you want to join the rebel traitor?"

"No, sir," said the private. "I will do as you command."

"That's better," said the guard. "You will report to me at sunrise tomorrow morning, and we will settle this affair. Now go!"

The private dashed through the door without another word. "Now bring in the boy," the guard said, turning to Rick.

"Remember," Rick said, glancing at Jim Davis, "he can't talk English, so it's no good ordering him to do anything. I'll be glad to translate." Jim Davis looked up in surprise. He looked first to Rick, to let him know he understood the game they were playing.

As Jim Davis looked to his friend, Danny Blackgoat, his eyes grew wide. He wrapped his arms around his bulky chest, letting Danny know the hug was meant for him. Danny pounded his chest in response.

The minds of these two men traveled to the same place—the front porch of the carpentry shop at Fort Davis, Texas. In the dark of night, while soldiers and the other prisoners had slept, Jim Davis had taught Danny the new language. He taught him to speak—and read—in the English language.

The voice of Major Henson ended their trip to the past.

"We have two prisoners today, two horse thieves," he said as he entered the officers' headquarters. Turning to Rick, he asked, "Does this boy know enough English to answer my questions?"

"He speaks mostly Navajo," said Rick, "but I can translate."

"Fine," said Major Henson. He gripped his hands behind his back and paced back and forth in front of the two prisoners. "You were a prisoner at Fort Davis, is that correct?" he asked Danny.

Danny looked to Rick, who spoke to him in the Navajo language. "Just nod and look at me, not Major Henson," Rick said. Danny kept his eyes on Rick and nodded.

"Good," said the major. "How did you escape?"

Once again Danny looked to Rick. "Talk to me in Navajo," Rick said. "Say anything you want, Danny. I know what to tell him."

"I want Jim Davis to live," said Danny. "Whatever you say, Jim Davis is innocent. Tell him."

Rick turned to the major. "He says he was afraid for his life," he said. "A prisoner tried to kill him, over and over. He even put a rattlesnake in his bed, and it bit him."

"Tell the boy he must answer the question!" Major Henson shouted. "How did you escape?" He grabbed the arms of Danny's chair and slid it hard against the wall. "I am losing my patience!"

"Just hang them both and be done with it," said Corporal Doyle.

"I will explain to him, Major Henson," said Rick. "I know you want the truth."

"That I do," said the major.

Rick turned once more to Danny. "Should I tell him of the graveyard?" he asked in Navajo.

"No," said Danny. "Jim Davis builds the coffins. That makes him more guilty."

"He says a good man gave him a horse and saved his life," Rick said to the major.

"Is this the good man who saved your life?" the major asked, pointing to Jim Davis but with his eyes still glued to Danny. "Does he know this good man stole the horse that saved his life? Does he know that we hang horse thieves?"

Danny looked back and forth, from Rick to Jim Davis to the major. He took a deep breath, stood up, and spoke in clear English.

"Major Henson," he said, "I want to confess. I stole the horse. I rode the horse from Fort Davis, as fast as I could. I came here to Fort Sumner because my family is here. This man is innocent," he said, looking at Davis. "He did not steal the horse. I did."

Chapter 21
Confession and the Hanging Rope

"Make sure he understands everything I am about to tell him," Major Henson said, looking to Rick.

"I understand everything you say," Danny said.

"Do you understand that you are confessing to a serious crime, stealing a horse?"

"Yes."

"Do you know the penalty for horse theft?" Danny looked to the floor and said nothing.

"The penalty is death by hanging," said the major.

"I stole the horse," Danny said. "Jim Davis is innocent. You cannot hang him."

Davis had been sitting quietly, trusting Rick to save his life any way he could. But when Danny confessed to the crime, Jim Davis could no longer stay silent.

"No!" he shouted, jumping to his feet. Corporal Doyle struck him in the ribs with the butt of his rifle, but Davis knocked the rifle away, ignoring the pain.

"This boy is lying," he said, pointing to Danny. "And you, Rick, how can you let him say this? He wants to give his life for me, but he is lying. I refuse to let him hang for my crime."

Doyle lifted his shotgun and aimed it at Davis. "Just say the word, Major Henson, and I will put an end to this." He cocked his gun and prepared to fire.

"Lower your weapon, Corporal," said Henson. "And you, Jim Davis. Sit down or you won't live to see the hanging rope."

Davis lowered himself to the bench, breathing hard and gripping his fists in anger. "Ask him where he got the horse," Davis said. "Go ahead, ask him!"

Danny stared at his friend with tears in his eyes. He felt hurt and betrayed.

"Enough of this," said Major Henson. "Rick, the noon hour is approaching. Bring your wagon to the hanging scaffold. Jim Davis will be first. We have two horse thieves today."

Rick rose slowly. "Jim Davis," he said, "do not do anything foolish. Please. The corporal is looking for a reason to shoot you. Do not let him have that pleasure."

"Shut up and do what you are told," said the corporal, glaring at Rick.

"Major," Rick asked, "will the general be there to witness the hanging?" He gave a quick glance at Davis as he spoke, raising his finger to his lips and letting Davis know he had a plan.

"Yes, every officer at Fort Davis will be present. That is our policy."

"I will see you in less than half an hour," Rick said, hurrying out the door. With the soldiers watching Rick depart, Jim Davis caught Danny's eye. He lifted his palm to his chest, so slowly no one noticed, then flipped his fingers open, as if tossing corn pollen to the morning sky.

He is telling me something, thought Danny. *Now is a time for me to pray and wait. I will not run or cause trouble.* With a quiet opening and closing of his eyes, he let Jim Davis know he understood.

"Let's go, both of you," said Major Henson. "Corporal Doyle, you lead the way, and keep your rifle at your side unless told otherwise."

As they stepped through the door, eight armed soldiers stood to greet them, waiting for orders. "I want three men on either side of the prisoners," barked the major, "and two will follow close behind. We will march in formation to the scaffold."

The soldiers were young and had never seen a hanging. They had never led condemned men to their death. They puffed out their chests and surrounded the prisoners, preparing to march.

"Yes, sir!" they shouted.

As they turned a corner, the hangman's noose came into sight. The scaffold it hung from stood tall and strong and weathered with age. The noose swung back and forth in the breeze, like a rattlesnake waiting for the time to strike.

At the sight of the hanging rope, Davis felt a stinging pain in his chest. He hunched over and took long, deep breaths. *Stay strong*, he said to himself. *Danny cannot help you now.* He was remembering the day when young Danny Blackgoat had pounded his chest, given him his own breath, and saved his life from a heart attack.

A soldier on horseback approached them. "The general will be here soon," the soldier said. "We are waiting only for the wagon."

"Let the general know we are ready when he gives the order," said Major Henson. "Do we have enough rope for another noose?"

"We have plenty of rope, Major Henson," the soldier said. "We have enough to hang them both."

Danny kept his eyes to the ground. He had made his choice. When he rode through the gate with Rick, he knew he might never leave Fort Sumner alive. But the news that both he and Jim Davis would hang stabbed him like a knife to the chest.

He closed his eyes and returned to the last day of happiness in his Navajo homeland. He saw himself climb the steep walls of the mesa near his home, as his sheep grazed in the canyon below. Danny remembered saying the morning prayer and pinching the corn pollen from the leather pouch he wore around his neck. For a brief moment, he saw streaks of deep red in the clouds to the east, as the sun lifted above the distant mountains.

But in a brief moment, his life forever changed, when soldiers rode into the neighborhood, firing shotguns and torching homes. Fiery clouds rose from the Navajo hogans as people fled from their homes. The soldiers herded the sheep into the corral behind Danny's home, then one by one led them to their slaughter. A soldier grabbed Danny and made him watch as he sliced the throat of Danny's favorite sheep, little Crowfoot.

"And I fought them every way I could," Danny whispered. "Till Jim Davis taught me how to win the battle by waiting and watching."

"Move on," said a soldier, poking Danny in the ribs. Danny jumped as if awakened from a dream world. He opened his eyes and looked around.

Jim Davis saved my life, he thought, *and it will cost him his own.*

A trumpet sounded, and General Bucknell, the fort commander, appeared, riding a high-stepping stallion and followed by twenty officers on horseback. He stepped from the saddle and saluted Major Henson and his men.

"Are we ready to proceed?" he asked.

"Yes, General Bucknell," Rick shouted, snapping the reins and driving his wagon to the hangman's noose. To the surprise of everyone, Rick stepped down from his wagon.

"General Bucknell," he said, "as the driver of the hanging wagon, I must speak to you, please."

"You have never been part of a hanging?" the general asked.

"No, but that is not the problem here."

"What is the problem?"

Rick approached General Bucknell in silence. He stood beside the general's horse before he finally spoke, so quietly no one else could hear.

"The two prisoners, Jim Davis and Danny Blackgoat, are charged with horse theft. They never stole the horse. My wife is Navajo. Danny Blackgoat is Navajo. She gave me her horse to save the young man's life."

"Are you telling me you gave Jim Davis the horse, the horse Danny Blackgoat rode during his escape?"

"Yes, General. I am guilty. You can charge me with offering a horse that allowed the boy to escape. Jim Davis is guilty of aiding the boy. Danny Blackgoat committed no crime, other than riding to Fort Sumner to be with his family."

"How do I know you are telling the truth?"

"If you check the underbelly of the horse," said Rick, "you will see he is not branded with the markings of a cavalry horse. He is a Navajo pony."

At that moment, a little girl rode her pony through the gates of the fort, screaming and waving her arms.

Chapter 22
Sarah Meets the General

"He didn't do it!" Sarah yelled. "Danny Blackgoat is innocent. Cut down the rope!"

General Bucknell stared at Rick, at first ignoring the scene behind him. He took a deep breath and slowly turned his head in the direction of the noise. He was greeted by the craziest scene he had ever seen in all of his thirty-five years in the United States Army. Four soldiers, waving their rifles with one hand and clutching their hats with the other, chased after a small girl racing through the gate and holding tight to the saddle horn of her pony.

"Mister Armyman General," Sarah shouted frantically, "that young man there is Danny

Blackgoat and he saved my life and my mother's and rescued us from slave traders and he is the best young man I ever met!"

General Bucknell lifted himself in the saddle and raised his right arm high, signaling to the soldiers. "Halt!" he said. "This girl presents no danger. I can take over from here."

The soldiers skidded to a stop and gave a quick salute to the general. "Yes, sir!" they said, and returned to the gate.

"Young lady," said the general, "I am in charge here."

"But, General, you can't—"

Bucknell smiled and touched his finger to his lips. "I talk first, you listen. Then you get to talk. Are you okay with that?"

Sarah nodded.

"First, who are you, and where are your parents?"

"My name is Sarah, and my parents are there," she said, pointing over her shoulder. Her mother and father stood by their horses, waiting at the gate.

"Let them enter!" Bucknell ordered. "Major Henson, before we continue with the hangings, we will hear what these people have to say. And you too, Rick. Follow me."

"General?" Rick asked.

"What is it?"

"May we bring Jim Davis and Danny Blackgoat with us? They have much to tell, all of which we can verify."

Soon the Gradys, Rick, Jim, and Danny were gathered in General Bucknell's office. "I would like to hear from you first, young man," the general said, nodding at Danny Blackgoat. "Take your time and tell me everything you remember, from the day you were first taken from your home."

Danny spoke for an hour, pausing as his story moved from the burning of his home and the death of his sheep. He told of being pulled away from his family and called a troublemaker when he tried to bring water to thirsty old people. He told the general about his trip to Fort Sumner, tied across the back of a horse. He described how Jim Davis helped him escape from Fort Davis, so he could be with his family. He also spoke of Sarah and the Grady family.

"They are good people," he said. "They fed me when I was hungry."

"And this young man, Danny Blackgoat, rescued my family," Mr. Grady added. "My wife and daughter were taken by slave traders, and many of my ranch workers were killed. But with Danny's help, we are alive and well."

Danny went on to tell the general about his nearby hideout at the rattlesnake cave, and how he carried fresh water to his family, to keep them alive.

General Bucknell sat silent for the entire hour, sipping his coffee and moving his gaze from one to the other. When Danny told of climbing from the coffin, the general noticed that Danny bowed his head—as if offering a prayer of thanks.

Finally, Sarah spoke, unable to contain herself any longer. "I rode my horse as fast as I could," she said, "to save the man who once saved me."

"And I am glad you did, young lady," General Bucknell said, rising slowly to his feet. "You prevented a grave injustice, and we are very thankful."

The unspoken question hung in the air. What happens now?

The general stepped from his office and spoke briefly to his officers. When he returned, his face had a serious look, but when he spotted Jim Davis his eyes softened. He stood beside him and waited for Davis to lift his face and look at him.

"Jim Davis," he said, "we still need a carpenter. What do you say?"

"I will be the best carpenter you've ever known," said Davis. "But a good carpenter needs a hardworking helper."

"I am glad you mentioned that. Would you mind training a young Navajo man to be your helper?"

"I would be honored," said Davis.

"Good. And Danny Blackgoat, you will be allowed to visit your family, to make sure they are safe. If you try to escape, I cannot promise your safety, or that of your family."

"I understand," Danny said. "I am here for my family."

"Now, Mr. and Mrs. Grady, I am sending six soldiers to accompany you home. They will camp out in the woods surrounding your ranch and be on the lookout for slave traders and villains. Will you agree to work with our soldiers, to give them sleeping quarters in bad weather, to cooperate with the US Army?"

"Yes, sir," Mr. Grady said. "And thank you for hearing all we had to say, especially my daughter Sarah."

"Rick," said General Bucknell, "you will remain here, at Fort Sumner, with your wife and family. No more dangerous journeys."

"Thank you," said Rick. "My wife will be very glad to hear that."

"You are welcome," said General Bucknell. "You will all stay in the soldiers' quarters tonight and say your good-byes in the morning. I will explain my final decision to my men, and they will follow my orders. No hangings today, and hopefully none for the remainder of your stay here."

As the morning sun rose on the following day, Danny Blackgoat stood on a hillside overlooking his family's campsite. But he was not alone. Standing close beside him, as she would for many years, stood Jane. He tossed corn pollen to the rising sun and offered once more his Navajo prayer.

When the morning sun casts its light on the canyon walls
A new house is born,
A house made of dawn.
Before me all is beautiful.
Behind me all is beautiful.
Above me all is beautiful.
Below me all is beautiful.
Around me all is beautiful.
Within me all is beautiful.

Tajahoteje.
Nothing will change.

Afterword:
Navajo Future,
the Treaty of 1868

In May 1868, General W. T. Sherman arrived at Fort Sumner to discuss the hardships and wishes of the Navajos. Chief Barboncito spoke for the Navajos.

"I was born at the lower end of Canyon de Chelly," he said. "We have been living here for five winters [at Fort Sumner] and have done all we possibly could to raise a crop of corn. This land does not like us. Neither does the water. In our country a rattlesnake gives a warning before he bites. We have all declared that we do not want to remain here any longer."

The following day, General Sherman agreed with the Navajos, adding, "Our government is determined that the enslavement of Navajos shall cease."

During five years of imprisonment, two thousand of the nine thousand Navajos who marched on the Long Walk from Navajo Nation to Fort Sumner died. The nearby lake was salt-filled, winters were brutal, and slave traders dragged hundreds from their families. Hearing that his people could now return to their homeland, Chief Barboncito was humble and joyful.

"After we get back to our country, the Navajos will be as happy as the land, black clouds will rise, and there will be plenty of rain. Corn will grow in abundance."

What happened to the Navajos in the 1860s was a terrible injustice. But unlike so many American Indians forced to leave their homelands, the Navajos were allowed to return. Struggles with land-grabbers, railroads, and treaty breakers continued, but the Navajos flourished—and today the Navajo Nation has the largest Indian population in America.

Recommended Resource

Diné: A History of the Navajos by Peter Iverson, with photos by Navajo photographer Monty Roessel.

About the Author

Tim Tingle is an Oklahoma Choctaw and an award-winning author and storyteller. Every Labor Day, Tingle performs a Choctaw story before the Choctaw chief's State of the Nation Address, a gathering that attracts over ninety thousand tribal members and friends.

In June 2011, Tingle spoke at the Library of Congress and presented his first performance at the Kennedy Center in Washington, DC. From 2011 to the present, he has been a featured author and storyteller at Choctaw Days, a celebration at the Smithsonian Institution's National Museum of the American Indian honoring the Oklahoma Choctaws.

Tingle's great-great-grandfather, John Carnes, walked the Trail of Tears in 1835. In 1992 Tim retraced the Trail to Choctaw homelands in Mississippi and began recording stories of tribal elders. His first book, *Walking the Choctaw Road*, was the outcome. His first children's book, *Crossing Bok Chitto*, garnered over twenty state and national awards and was an Editor's Choice in the *New York Times* Book Review.

As an instructor at the University of Oklahoma, Tingle presented summer classes in Santa Fe, New Mexico. Fueled by his own family's survival on the Trail of Tears, he became fascinated with the Navajo Long Walk, and the Danny Blackgoat series came to life.

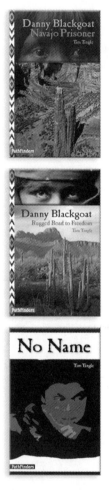

Danny Blackgoat: Navajo Prisoner
Tim Tingle
978-1-93905-303-9
$9.95 • 144 pages

Danny Blackgoat: Rugged Road to Freedom
Tim Tingle
978-1-93905-305-3
$9.95 • 176 pages

No Name
Tim Tingle
978-1-93905-306-0
$9.95 • 168 pages